Doubting Heart

Lenny kissed me, and I kissed him back, my heart aching because I had caused him so much pain. But try as I might, I couldn't feel sure of my love for him anymore. My lips were kissing him, but my head and my heart felt curiously detached, like I was only going through the motions.

Lenny must have sensed how I felt, because he pulled away from me. "It's not working, is it? You don't love me anymore, do you?"

It felt awful to hear him say it like that. I didn't want to hurt him more, but I knew I had to be honest. "I don't know, Lenny, I just don't know. I still care for you, I really do! But I can't swear I still love you, because if I did, I don't know if I could still feel the way I do about Dave. I'm so confused. I just don't know what to do . . ."

"What to do? The choice is clear to me, Linda. You can still have me if you want me, but you're going to have to end it with Dave. You can't be my girl and keep seeing him, too."

Books by Linda Lewis

2 YOUNG
2 GO
---
4 BOYS

WANT TO TRADE TWO BROTHERS FOR A CAT?

Available from MINSTREL Books

WE HATE EVERYTHING BUT BOYS
IS THERE LIFE AFTER BOYS?
WE LOVE ONLY OLDER BOYS
MY HEART BELONGS TO THAT BOY
ALL FOR THE LOVE OF THAT BOY
DEDICATED TO THAT BOY I LOVE
LOVING TWO IS HARD TO DO

Available from ARCHWAY Paperbacks

Loving Two
Is Hard To Do

Linda Lewis

AN ARCHWAY PAPERBACK
Published by POCKET BOOKS
New York   London   Toronto   Sydney   Tokyo   Singapore

AN ARCHWAY PAPERBACK *Original*

An Archway Paperback published by
POCKET BOOKS, a division of Simon & Schuster Inc.
1230 Avenue of the Americas, New York, NY 10020

ISBN-13: 978-1-416-97534-2
ISBN-10: 1-416-97534-9

First Archway Paperback printing June 1990

10 9 8 7 6 5 4 3 2 1

AN ARCHWAY PAPERBACK and colophon are
registered trademarks of Simon & Schuster Inc.

Printed in the U.S.A.

IL 7+

To Roz and Fay
and all the kids on the park wall

Chapter

One

I KEPT WAITING FOR SOMETHING HORRIBLE TO HAPPEN. THE air was thick with tension as we all sat at the round table—Lenny Lipoff, the boy I loved; my parents, strict, old-fashioned, and totally against my relationship with Lenny; Ira and Joey, my pesty twin brothers, who liked nothing better than to stir up trouble between everyone; and me.

"You can order anything you want, Lenny, so don't be shy," my mother said, and I gazed at her in amazement. True, this was a special occasion. It was not only my seventeenth birthday, but my graduation from high school as well. Still, I had never expected my parents to invite Lenny out to a restaurant to celebrate with our family.

"Don't say that to him—now he's sure to order the most expensive thing on the menu," Joey said nastily.

I would have loved to kick him under the table, but he was sitting too far away for me to reach. It was hard to believe my brothers were thirteen years old now,

Linda Lewis

official teenagers. While Ira, who had recently developed an interest in girls, showed occasional flashes of maturity, Joey was still an absolute baby, and a bratty one at that.

"Now, Joseph." My father's bushy eyebrows drew together in a warning frown. As much as he disliked Lenny, my father was not about to let my brothers ruin this family dinner.

"It's all right, Mr. Berman. I've been around the twins long enough now to have learned not to take anything they say seriously," Lenny said good-naturedly.

"You sure have been around long enough!" Ira piped in. "Three years of going out with Linda—unbelievable!"

"Unbelievably disgusting, if you ask me," Joey couldn't resist adding.

"No one asked you anything, big mouth," I reminded him.

"How's everybody doing? Ready to order?" Fortunately, our smiling, redheaded waitress arrived on the scene. That ended the discussion before it could lead to any serious disturbances.

Actually, as much as I hated to admit it, my brother Ira was right, I couldn't help thinking as the waitress went around the table taking everyone's orders. It was unbelievable that Lenny and I had been going together for almost three years. In the beginning, I don't think anyone would have given us three weeks.

I was the kind of kid who didn't get into trouble. I was a serious student, and serious about my future, too. I guess it was because my parents had always hammered into my head the importance of getting a good education that I did so well in school. At any rate, I graduated high school a year early, with honors, and would be attending Barnard College in the fall.

Lenny, on the other hand, was constantly in trouble of one sort or another, and his school history was a complete disaster. It wasn't that he wasn't smart enough—Lenny was a great reader of newspapers, magazines, encyclopedias, almanacs, and history books, and he absorbed everything that interested him. He had done fine in school when he was younger and could get by on brains alone. But once he started high school, things had gotten so bad for him at home that he was unable to discipline himself to concentrate on schoolwork. He had started cutting classes and failing courses. Finally, in his junior year, he was kicked out of school.

Lenny was an only child and came from a broken home. His parents never got along, and there was always so much tension, screaming, and fighting in his house that he found it unbearable to be there. His parents eventually separated, but that didn't stop Lenny's mother from fighting with him. Things had deteriorated to where right before Christmas Lenny had joined the navy.

I had been devastated when he told me the news. But as we talked about it I realized it was probably the best thing he could have done. Lenny had been going through some tough times in the city. He couldn't get a decent job without a high school diploma, and his relationship with his mother was so bad she was about to throw him out of the house. The navy would give him a chance to straighten up and to get an education and a career. It would be hard for me to be away from him, but if things worked out and Lenny got himself together, it would be well worth it. By the time he got out of the navy I would be almost finished with college, and, I hoped, we would be able to get married.

This was not a hope my parents shared with me. They didn't like the fact that Lenny had so many problems and that he hadn't done well in school. All the fights, breakups, and makeups we had had when we were first going together and the hurts I had suffered trying to help him through his ups and downs served to make them dislike him more.

I didn't like my parents' attitude, but I couldn't really blame them for it. Lenny's faults were on the surface, there for them to see clearly; his good points were a lot less obvious. My parents never got to see Lenny at his softer, more tender moments, when his common sense and depth of feeling prevailed. I could talk to Lenny about things I never could with anyone else and listen to his mesmerizing voice for hours. Lenny was fun to be with, and so full of life he breathed excitement into everything he did. And then there was a powerful physical attraction between us I never could resist. I certainly couldn't expect my parents to understand that.

But at the moment I wasn't trying to get them to understand anything. All I wanted was to get through dinner without any disasters!

Maybe it was because this was such a special occasion. Maybe it was because Lenny was leaving in the morning to go back to the naval school in Florida, or because he announced to my parents that he just found out he had passed his test for his high school equivalency diploma, so in a sense this was his graduation, too. Or maybe it was because my brothers were so busy eating that they didn't have time to make too many snotty remarks. At any rate, except for the fact that clumsy Ira knocked over his water glass and splattered Joey's food, there actually were no disasters during dinner. Not only that, my parents invited Lenny to come back to our house for a while. Of course, with all the rules and regulations they set up, like no closing doors and sitting only on chairs, not on the bed, there was no privacy in my apartment. But at least my parents were showing some acceptance.

The best part of the evening came when it was time for Lenny to go, and I walked him out into the hallway of my apartment building to say goodbye. Finally we were alone! We stood on the staircase between the second-and third-floor landings, a spot where people almost never passed by, and he took me into his arms. He kissed me, and I immediately felt that powerful magnetic force between us that never failed to take my breath away. It was stronger than ever now that I knew I wouldn't be seeing him for so long.

I gazed at him, trying to etch every detail of the way he looked into my memory. I touched his brown hair that curled around his adorable baby face. I traced with my finger his high cheekbones, his fine, aquiline nose, his sensuous lips. I stared into his warm brown eyes fringed with lashes that were long and straight. "Oh, Lenny, I'll miss you so much while we're apart," I said.

"I hope so. I'd hate to think you might find someone else while you're away working in the country."

"Lenny! How can you say something like that? You know I'm completely loyal to you. I'm not interested in finding anyone else. I love you!"

"And I love you, Linda. You're the best—so bright and sweet and pretty, with your perfect little body,

5

and those incredible big blue eyes. I guess that's why I always worry that some fast-talking lover boy will come along and sweep you off your feet."

I had to laugh at that. "I've already got a fast-talking lover boy—you!"

He didn't laugh back. "I'm serious, Linda. You'll find that working at a hotel in New Hampshire is totally different from being home in New York City. You'll be on your own, with lots of freedom, and there will be plenty of college boys there with their minds set on one thing. Being in the country is very romantic, and I'd hate to think of you there on some moonlit summer night succumbing to—"

"Lenny! I'm not succumbing to anything—except my love for you, that is. I don't even need romantic surroundings for that—it can happen right here in this dingy hallway. I'll show you."

I kissed him then, with such passion that he had to believe me. I loved him so much that I didn't want to think that it would be two long months before we could be together again, maybe longer if he couldn't get leave from the navy. How I wished that I never had to part from him, that we could hold and kiss and love each other all night long, then on and on forever and ever.

There was nothing to compare with this love I had for Lenny—nothing. We had gone through so much together, I was sure that no one would ever come between us.

There was no way of knowing then that I was wrong.

Chapter
Two

LENNY WAS GONE. I MISSED HIM TERRIBLY, BUT AT LEAST I had getting ready for the country to keep me busy. Before I knew it, it was Saturday, and I was saying goodbye to my parents and to New York City. Then I was on the bus, heading for New Hampshire and my summer job at the Grandview Hotel.

I owed this job to Roz Buttons, who had been one of my very best friends for years and years. The two of us were to run the preschool camp group for children of the guests at the Grandview, and we were to be roommates as well. Roz had been the one to find out about the job, and she convinced me to come along by promising the work would be easy, the place would be beautiful, and we would have a terrific summer.

I wasn't sure about how the summer would go, but Roz was right about the place being beautiful. The New Hampshire mountains were gorgeous, the countryside dotted with majestic forests and quaint little villages and farms. And the Grandview was lovely, three large white clapboard buildings with big porches, surrounded by grassy fields, woodlands, and mountains.

"Linda! I'm so glad you're here!" Already tanned and looking bouncy and pretty with her honey-colored hair swept back from her face, Roz was there to greet me as I got off the bus. She had come to the country several days earlier with her parents, who were spending a week's vacation at the hotel. "Let's take your things to our room and dump them. Then I'll fill you in on everything!"

I followed Roz into one of the white buildings and up three flights of stairs. "This floor is just for staff," she said when we finally reached the top. "Our room's at the end of the hall."

Our room was small, with nothing more in it than a bed, chair, and dresser for each of us, but the view of the mountains from the window near my bed was spectacular. How I wished Lenny could be there to see it with me. If only he had had a normal life and gone to college instead of the navy, he could have gotten a summer job at the Grandview, too, and we could have had a fabulously romantic summer together.

"Dump your stuff on the bed for now—you can unpack later," Roz interrupted my thoughts. "I want time to show you around and set up for the start of camp before dinner."

As we walked outside Roz told me I was one of the last staff members to arrive. "The kids that work here come mostly from New York or from Boston. The girls seem nice, and there are some guys that are positively gorgeous! I've got my eye on this waiter named Mel. He's got the sexiest eyes I've ever seen, so just control yourself when you meet him. You can have your pick of the rest, though," she said with a laugh.

"Roz! You know I'm not interested in any other boys! Lenny and I have an agreement to be loyal to each other. We consider ourselves to be practically engaged."

"Oh, come off it, Linda. 'Practically engaged' means nothing. Until there's a ring sitting on the fourth finger of your left hand, you're still a free agent, open to any boy who comes along. You know how I feel about your relationship with Lenny—it's crazy for you to be tied down at age seventeen. This summer is a wonderful opportunity to live a little and open yourself to meeting someone else and seeing what you're missing!"

"Okay, Roz, we've taken this subject far enough," I sighed. Ever since she had broken up with her first boyfriend, Sheldon, and started dating others, Roz had been pressuring me to break up with Lenny and do the same. She couldn't understand the concept of loving someone so much you really didn't want to go out with anyone else. Roz and I had had similar discussions in the past, and they hadn't led anywhere. I didn't want to get into it again. "Why don't you fill me in on what's what around here?" I said.

Roz took me out and showed me the tennis courts, the lake, and the main building where meals were served. Then she cut across the field next to the swimming pool. "This is the pool," she stated. "And the guy standing near it is Dave. Let's go over and I'll introduce you. He's really cute."

Roz headed to the pool, and I had no choice but to follow her. The sun was shining in my eyes as I approached him, and it was only by squinting that I could make out his short but bronzed and muscular body, clad only in a white bathing suit, his dark hair and eyes, his rugged, even features. I shifted my angle so I could see him better. Roz was right, he was really cute.

"Dave Balen, I want you to meet my friend, Linda Berman, who's going to help me run the kiddy camp group," Roz said. "Dave's the social and athletic director here this summer, Linda."

"What exactly does that mean?" I was surprised to hear the shakiness in my voice as I asked the question.

"It means I plan the activities to make sure the guests have a good time." He smiled, showing teeth that were white and even. "Exciting stuff like dance lessons and parties around the pool, Ping-Pong and tennis tournaments, dart-throwing contests."

He had this cute tang to his voice I wasn't used to hearing. "Wow! I didn't know it was possible for life to be that exciting. Are your activities only for the guests, or can we staff members participate, too?"

"We're allowed to do whatever we want when we're off duty," Dave answered. "Swim, go boating, dance. There's a great band that plays every night in the rec hall. Do you like to dance?"

"I love to."

"Great! Then I'll meet you in the rec hall tonight, and we'll dance until the band quits playing."

Before I could answer that I didn't think it would be right for me to meet him because I had this boyfriend I was committed to in the city, we were interrupted by the arrival of another boy in a bathing suit. He was dark with curly hair, and, in contrast to Dave, he was huge—well over six feet tall and solidly built. He reminded me of an enormous grizzly bear.

"Have you met our lifeguard, Perry Sutowski, Linda?" Dave asked. "He's from New York, too."

"No. I just got off the bus from the city, and you guys are the first people I've laid eyes on."

"Well, now that you've met us, there's no one else you need to know." Perry grinned. "We'll be seeing lots of each other, especially since Dave and I share the room down the hall from you and Roz."

"Oh. That's—uh—nice." My eyes met Dave's, and I found him looking at me intently. He didn't break his gaze until Perry put his arm on him and pulled him away.

"Come on, Dave. You've got to help me set up the pool."

"Oh. Sure, Perry. See you tonight then, Linda."

Again I wanted to tell him that I really couldn't because I already had a boyfriend, but now it was Roz who interfered. "We'll be there. But right now we've got some setting up of our own to do. We've got tons to do before kiddy camp starts tomorrow. Come on, Linda. See you later, guys!"

I barely had time to wave goodbye before Roz was dragging me down the path that led to the kiddy camp building. Right before we disappeared into the woods I turned around and found that Dave was still staring after me.

Tucked into a clearing and surrounded by a playground complete with the usual swings, slide, sandbox, and assorted climbing devices, the kiddy camp building was a cute little cottage set up like a nursery school. The guests at the Grandview could send all children aged three to six to kiddy camp, where Roz and I would keep them busy while the parents lounged around the pool or took part in Dave's social and athletic activities.

I had worked at camps before, and I had plenty of experience baby-sitting for and tutoring kids, but this was the first time I was responsible for a group of my own. I wanted to plan out and structure a schedule for the entire day before the kids arrived. Roz thought we should wait to see what the kids were like first and take it from there. We compromised by having a few planned activities, such as swimming, an arts and crafts project each day, and a music and story-telling period; the rest of the time we would have the kids choose activities on their own. Having come to this agreement, Roz and I got busy unpacking crayons, paints, books, puzzles, and clay, and placing them on the shelves in preparation for start of camp.

"So what did you think of Dave?" Roz asked as we worked. "Cute, isn't he? From the moment I first met him I knew he'd be perfect for you. And he liked you, too—I could see it in the way he stared into your big baby-blues! It really was a riot to observe the whole scene!"

"What 'whole scene' are you talking about, Roz?" I asked irritably. "Dave happens to be cute, but so what? Might I remind you one more time that I am going with Lenny and not interested in any other boy?"

"Okay, okay. Forget I even mentioned that you and Dave would make a very attractive couple," Roz said. Then I guess she noticed the dirty look I was giving her, because she changed the subject. "How about if we put out some crayons and paper for the kids to color when they first come in?"

"Good idea. I'll put some puzzles out, too." As I

was sorting through the puzzles, trying to decide which might be appropriate for the kids that were scheduled to arrive, a loud knocking was heard on the door.

"Go away! Camp doesn't start until tomorrow!" Roz called out.

"But I want to come today!" said this high-pitched voice. The door opened, and Dave peered in. He squatted down to kid height and waddled over to the table. He grabbed a puzzle and started to put it together, then pretended to be having trouble. He looked up at me and, in the same falsetto, pleaded, "Help me, help me. This is so hard, counselor—uh, what did you say your name was?"

I couldn't help laughing. "Linda. And it's only hard because you picked something far too difficult for your age and intelligence. Here, try this." I handed him a puzzle with only four pieces: triangle, circle, square, and rectangle, each in different colors.

"That's too hard, too." Dave pushed it away, then grabbed my hand and pulled me closer to him. He stared at me and, with his voice back to normal, said, "The only puzzle I want to figure out now is you."

"Me?" I laughed nervously and pulled my hand away. "I'm no puzzle. What do you want to know about me?"

"Oh . . . everything." He smiled his dazzling smile. "I'm finished helping Perry, so I figured this would be a good time to get to know you better. So start at the day you were born and fill me in on every detail until the moment I saw you standing by the pool."

Somewhat overwhelmed by this, I looked over to Roz for assistance. She was no help at all. "This is a story I've heard already, so if you don't mind, I'll go arrange stuff out in the playground while you two get to know each other," she said laughingly.

"But—" Before I could get out my planned words of protest, Roz was already out the door. Defeated, I sank down in the chair next to Dave. He really seemed interested, and I didn't suppose there was any harm in relating the kinds of things he wanted to know.

I told Dave that I had grown up in Washington Heights, a neighborhood of concrete and brick apartment buildings in the upper Manhattan part of New York City. I told him about my pain-in-the-neck brothers, Ira and Joey. I told him that I was looking forward to starting Barnard College in September. I was about to tell him about Lenny when he broke in.

"So you're going to Barnard. Good school, but it's right in the city, isn't it? I'm a firm believer that everyone should go away to school. I do, myself, even though there are plenty of good schools in Boston, where I come from. I'm a history major—prelaw, actually. I'm a junior at U. Mass.—that's the University of Massachusetts at Amherst. Great school. Great social life. I live in a fraternity house, and there are swinging parties every weekend."

"Massachusetts, huh? I guess that explains your accent. I never heard anyone say 'BAHnahd College' before," I giggled.

"Accent! You think I have an accent? Why, I knew you were from New York from the moment you opened your mouth!"

"Oh, yeah? Well, then why did you bother asking me questions about myself, since you already knew all the answers?"

He reached out and unexpectedly grabbed my hand

again. "I don't think I could ever know enough about you. Tell me more."

He gazed into my eyes when he said that and leaned over so that his face was right near mine. I was so overwhelmed by the nearness of him that it took me a while to come to my senses and pull away. I knew I had to tell him about Lenny immediately.

"Well, the thing that's most important for you to know is that I have a boyfriend back home," I said quickly. "His name is Lenny, and we've been going together for three years now, and we're very serious."

"Oh, is that so? And is he coming up here to the Grandview this summer?"

"No, I don't see how he can. He's in the navy and probably won't be getting any more leave for some time."

"Good. Then we won't have to do much worrying about him, will we?" Dave took my hand again and grinned.

"Hey! Cut it out!" I jerked away from him. Then I felt foolish at my overreaction. After all, I didn't want Dave to think I disliked him or anything. "I mean I just wanted to make sure you understand I'm already spoken for. We could still be good friends," I told him, smiling to make sure he knew there was nothing personal in my rejection.

"Sure, I understand," he said. But I could tell by the way he looked at me that those words didn't mean anything to him at all.

Chapter

Three

I HAD GRAVE DOUBTS ABOUT WHETHER OR NOT IT WAS WISE
to show up at the rec hall that night, but Roz convinced me it was the thing to do.

"You've got to come, Linda. The rec hall's the place
where all the kids who work at the Grandview have a
chance to get together. All the waiters, waitresses, and
busboys will be there. We hang out in the back, get free
sodas, kid around, and dance. It's great fun, and if you
don't come, there will be nothing to do but stay in our
room by yourself. You'll be considered an outcast by
everyone. Besides, I want you to meet Mel, the boy
I've got my eye on for this summer's romance. I need
you there for moral support."

Once Roz put it that way, I really couldn't refuse. I
certainly didn't want to spend the summer as an
outcast, sitting alone in my room each night. I began
to get ready, changing from the shorts and T-shirt I
had worn during the day to my favorite pair of jeans
and a good blouse. I ran a comb through my shoulder-

length light brown hair and put on just enough makeup to bring out the blue of my eyes.

"You look great!" Roz said as she looked me over. "Those jeans really emphasize your figure. Petite but adorable."

"Thanks," I said gratefully. Roz, who knew how to dress for any occasion, was blessed with smooth, clear skin and honey-colored hair and eyes. Although she was as short as I was, her body had developed curves in all the right places to give her a very sexy appearance. A compliment from her was worth something.

Still, I was somewhat nervous as I followed Roz into the rec hall, a large room with tables where people could sit, eat, and drink. In the front was a stage where the hotel's band played popular music, and also an area for dancing.

"The back table in the corner is reserved for staff," Roz told me as she led me in that direction. I saw some college-age kids I didn't know sitting there, and I hung back a bit shyly. But there was nothing shy about Roz. In the two days she had spent in the country before my arrival she seemed to have gotten to know everyone.

"I'd like you all to meet my friend, Linda," she announced breezily. "Linda, this is Cindy, Alice, and Karla, all waitresses. The guys, who are either waiters or busboys, are Jim, Harvey, John, and"—she paused and took a deep breath before she said the last name—"this is Mel Rhodes."

I looked at Mel, and it was easy to see why Roz was attracted to him. He really was good-looking, with dark, curly hair, thick eyebrows, and eyes that were deep and blue. But you could tell by the conceited air

17

he had about him that he was fully aware of his good looks, and that turned me off. I never cared much for boys who were so in love with themselves that they had no interest in anyone else. My initial instinct was that Roz was on the road to heartbreak if she fell for Mel.

"Hi, Linda. Come join our group." Mel moved aside so that Roz and I could squeeze in next to him. Roz struck up a conversation with him immediately, and I was left to listen to it, plus the bits and pieces of other conversations that floated to me from around the table. No one was talking to me directly.

Feeling a bit awkward and out of place, I tuned out the conversations and listened instead to the music. The band was playing an old, slow Beatles song I loved, and I found myself rhythmically moving and swaying.

"Hey, how about standing up and doing that together with me?" a male voice asked. It was Dave, smiling at me, his hand outstretched. I took it and got up to dance with him. I did love to dance, and by that time I was happy to leave the group at the table that seemed to have no interest in me.

Dave took me into his arms and led me across the dance floor with such skill that I was surprised. I guess that was because I was so used to Lenny, who really didn't like to dance and only went through the motions to please me.

I was a little over five feet tall, and Dave was probably only five or six inches taller, but this proved an asset when it came to dancing with me. His movements were strong and sure, yet gentle. We glided together comfortably, true partners in our motions, as if dancing was something we had done together many times in the past.

"I knew we'd be great together." Dave smiled at me when the music ended.

"We do seem to *dance* well together," I replied.

"How about another?" he asked as the band began another song, a fast one this time.

"Sure, why not?" There obviously was no harm in a fast dance. We hardly touched each other, just moved to the music, separate and yet together, and aware of each other's presence the entire time.

When that dance was over there was another fast song, and another slow one followed. By that time it seemed to be taken for granted that Dave and I would be dancing together for as long as the band kept playing, and I seemed to be firmly affixed in his arms.

I was so comfortable that I let my head rest on his shoulder. I found myself closing my eyes.

That's when I felt a tapping on my back and heard my name repeated frantically. My eyes flew open, and I saw the interruption was caused by Roz.

"Linda," she said, "the desk clerk just came in and said he was looking all over for you. There's a long-distance call for you, person to person, and supposedly very urgent. Can you get to the phone right away?"

"Phone? Urgent?" I blinked, for I hadn't been expecting anyone to call. And then I realized who was the only one who could be calling me. "Lenny!" I said aloud. "It's got to be Lenny!"

I took the call in the upstairs corridor right outside my room. I figured I would have more privacy there than by the noisy front desk.

Linda Lewis

"Hello?" I was all out of breath from running.

"Hi, baby." The sound of Lenny's voice was enough to send shivers through me. "What took you so long to get to the phone?"

"I was in the rec hall. They wouldn't interrupt the band by using the loudspeaker system in there, so the desk clerk had to come find me in person."

"Rec hall? What's that?"

"A room where they have social activities like dancing to a live band each night to entertain the guests. That's where the kids who work here hang out."

"Oh. And whom were you dancing with?"

"Oh, mostly with this guy Dave." I hoped my voice sounded casual and unaffected. "He's a junior at U. Mass. and has the job of social director for the summer. He loves to dance."

"Oh, he does, does he? And does he know that you're already taken—by me?"

"Of course, Lenny. I tell everyone I have a boyfriend right away so nobody will get the wrong idea. There's nothing between Dave and me."

"There better not be. I don't want to have to leave the navy and come up to New Hampshire to take care of some punk from Massachusetts who tries to steal my girl!"

"Don't be silly, Lenny," I said nervously. "You know I'm completely loyal. Now tell me what's going on with you. What is it that was so urgent?"

"Urgent? Oh, that was just my way of getting them to make sure to find you. There's really nothing much going on here. School's as tedious and boring as ever. Communications sounds like a good field, but the more I get into it, the more I don't like it. Sometimes I think the only reason I continue with it is to prove to you that I can finish something successfully."

His words were very upsetting to me. It was true that I had put high hopes on Lenny's making it in this school and being able to get a good job when he got out, but I didn't want him to be miserable because of it. "I know you can finish something successfully," I answered. "You got through boot camp, and you got your equivalency diploma, too. I'd like to see you get through this school, but it's got to be because you want it, Lenny. That's something you've got to decide for yourself."

"Well, I've decided to .stick it out—for now, at least, until I can come up with a better idea. I can handle things here as long as I know you're being good and loyal and all that stuff up there in the country."

"I am, I am," I promised. "As far as I'm concerned, I'm only working here to earn some money and pass the time until we can be together again."

"That's great to hear! I've got to go now. Remember I love you."

"I love you, too." I stood there holding on to the receiver even after I heard the dial tone. Speaking to Lenny made me feel guilty about how much I had been enjoying the time with Dave.

"So there really is a Lenny. And you really do fancy yourself in love with him."

Startled, I whirled around when I heard the voice. There was Dave standing behind me, this strange look on his face. How much of my conversation had he overheard? "W-what are you doing here, Dave?" I asked.

"Well, the desk clerk said the call was urgent, so I figured I would make sure that everything's all right."

"Everything's fine. That was Lenny, my boyfriend, calling me from the navy."

"Oh. And did he say anything about coming up here to see you?"

"No. He can't. He's going to school in Florida."

"Good. Then we can continue to do as we please." He grinned impishly.

"Dave! I told you Lenny and I were serious!"

"Sure you did. But right now he's where he is, and we're here. So why don't we enjoy ourselves and do some more dancing?"

Part of me felt that it was wrong to be enjoying myself when Lenny was stuck there in the navy, but another part of me did not. After all, how would it benefit Lenny for me to be unhappy? Dancing was a harmless activity, and I might as well have as good a time as possible this summer.

I went back to the rec hall with Dave.

Lenny wrote me almost every other day and called me at least once a week. Things didn't seem to be getting any better in school, but he was still hanging in there. He missed me terribly and longed for the day we could be together again.

I missed him, too, but I was enjoying my work in the country. On nice days, with swimming, boating, fishing, and playing outside on the playground equipment, the time went by fast. Rainy days were more difficult, as we were stuck in the kiddy camp building, trying to keep anywhere from six to twelve kids busy indoors. Usually Dave and Perry, who didn't have much to do when it rained, would come to our rescue by showing a movie in the rec hall, and we would take the kids to see it.

Camp lasted until three in the afternoon; then Roz and I were off until five-thirty. We ate our meals with the kids in the children's dining room and then were responsible for them until seven-thirty, when the adults finished dinner. The rest of the evening was our own. Sometimes there was an adult movie at night, or a bingo game, or a special show that we could go to. There was always dancing in the rec hall, or sometimes a group of kids would get together and walk the few blocks into town to get something to eat at Sam's Café or Tony's Pizza. There we would meet up with kids who worked at some of the other hotels in the area.

Wherever I went, Dave always managed to make an appearance. He would stop off at kiddy camp to joke around whenever he had a spare moment. He would invite me for dance lessons at the pool during my time off. He would offer to buy me sodas or ice cream or pizza and suggest we take long walks together to watch the sunset. He was always smiling, always pleasant, always attentive, and he made it perfectly clear he'd like to get something going with me, if only I would give him the chance.

I have to admit I was flattered by his attention. It was a long time since I had been pursued by anyone, and Dave was a college boy, a future lawyer, and good-looking, too. Besides, I liked him. We had great conversations together, and a lot of fun. As long as I kept reminding him that I was serious about Lenny and was only interested in friendship from anyone else, I figured I had the situation under control.

I figured wrong. It didn't matter to Dave that I had a boyfriend. "I know all about Lenny," he would say when I reminded him of the fact because he was still holding my hand long after the dance we had been dancing had ended. "But there's nothing wrong with holding hands—it's a friendly thing to do."

"Well, as long as you know it's only because we're friends." Eventually I gave in to him and let him hold my hand. I didn't want to make Dave feel bad, and I really did like holding hands with him. The physical contact gave me a nice, warm feeling of closeness.

Of course, once I went along with hand-holding, it was that much harder to say no to other forms of physical contact. What was the harm if he put his arm around my chair while the movie was showing? What was the harm if he put his arm around me when we walked to Sam's Café?

It was the night that Roz finally made a connection with gorgeous Mel Rhodes that things started changing. It was more than two weeks since camp had begun, and Roz had been working on getting Mel to notice her the entire time. A group of us had gone together to Sam's, and she had managed to wind up sitting next to Mel and sharing an ice cream sundae with him. I was glad to see them getting on so well, because I knew how much Roz liked him. After a while Roz came over to me and said, "I have to go to the ladies' room, Linda. Want to go, too?"

I was about to tell her that if I needed the ladies' room, I was quite capable of getting there on my own, when I noticed the expression of urgency on her face. It took me a while, but I realized she needed to talk to me. I followed her to the ladies' room in the back.

Roz closed the door behind us and checked the stalls to make sure we were alone. "Linda! You've got to do me the greatest favor in the world!"

"I do? And what's that?"

"Stay out of our room for a while. Mel has agreed to come up there with me, and I want some time alone with him."

"Stay out of our room? But it's almost eleven o'clock, Roz, and I'm already getting tired. Where am I supposed to go so late?"

"Well, the band plays till midnight, and there's always someone hanging around to dance. And then I thought maybe you could hang out at Dave and Perry's room."

"What? Are you crazy, Roz? They're boys, you know!"

"Of course I know. But they're good guys—you can trust them not to try anything you wouldn't want them to do. And this is so important to me, Linda. Pl-eease! I may never get a chance like this with Mel again."

I was about to tell her that if this was her only chance with Mel, their relationship couldn't be worth very much, but I thought better of it. Roz had been obsessed with Mel ever since her first day at the Grandview, and she was counting on me to help her do what she thought she needed to do to get him. If I said no and it didn't work out for her, she'd never forgive me.

"Okay, Roz. The room is yours until midnight. After that I'm coming up to sleep."

She hugged me. "Thanks, Linda. You always were a great friend."

"Don't worry, I'll keep you company," Dave assured me when Sam's closed up, and I told him why my room was off limits. "Why don't we go sit by the pool? It's a beautiful night, and those lounge chairs are really comfortable."

I hesitated. I remembered Lenny's warning to me about romantic moonlit summer nights. But everyone else was gone already, and I certainly didn't want to spend this time by myself. I had always been able to keep Dave under control before. "Okay," I agreed. "But keep in mind that this is just another 'friendly' thing to do."

"Of course," he replied. "Although I'm beginning to think that my name is 'just friends'—you say it to me so often."

"I have to be sure you don't get the wrong idea," I said. With that warning, I let him take my hand and lead me along the dark path to the pool.

As Dave had noted, it really was a beautiful night. The moon was a round silver ball, and the stars sparkled against the backdrop of mountain peaks opening up to the endless sky. Dave had the key to the pool storage area, and he got us cushions for the lounge chairs and thick towels to ward off the chill of the night.

We each took a lounge and lay back, watching the stars and listening to the sound of the band playing the last few songs of the evening. Then the only music was the sounds of the country night—the chirping of the crickets, the hooting of an owl, the rustling of the leaves in the summer breeze. The rest of the hotel was sleeping. There was only Dave and me.

I let him hold my hand because it felt good to do so. We talked softly of small things that had happened during the day, and then we were silent. I was very aware of the nearness of him, and yet of the separation between us that had to be.

The New Hampshire night grew colder, and I shivered even under the thick towel.

"Cold?" Dave picked up on this right away.

"Uh-huh." I shivered again. "I guess it's because I've been still for so long."

"Why don't you come sit with me, and I'll warm you up?"

"With you? In your chair?"

"Yup. I won't bite you, you know. You'll have the heat from my body, and we'll put both towels over us. Come on. I'm getting chilly myself."

"Okay." I climbed into Dave's chair and leaned back against him. He threw the towels over me and wrapped his arms around me as well. It really was a lot warmer that way.

He put his face up against my hair, and I could hear his soft breathing. We were no closer together than we were when we danced, but somehow we seemed to be. There was something so intimate and romantic about the two of us being alone together in the moonlight. It scared me; sometimes I had feelings for Dave I didn't want to have at all.

I forced myself to think of other things. I wondered what Lenny was doing just then. I wondered what Roz was doing with Mel up in our room. Was she kissing him, right this moment? It had been weeks since the last time I had been kissed. How I missed the touch of Lenny's lips against mine, the wonderful feeling of being in his arms. How long would it be until I could be together with him once again?

I guess I must have sighed aloud because Dave

heard me. "What's the matter, little girl?" he whispered tenderly.

"I guess the vastness of the night makes me feel lonely," I admitted.

"There's no reason for you to be lonely when you're here with me," he answered. He tightened his hold around me, and I felt him kissing my hair and my cheek.

"Don't," I protested, rolling back my head to get away from him. But that exposed my neck to him, and he began kissing me there.

"Please, Linda, it's only a kiss," he whispered into my hair. His voice was so full of longing, it cried out to and touched the loneliness that ached inside of me. I felt myself giving in to him. It was only a kiss. It wouldn't hurt anyone. And it felt so good.

Chapter

Four

I HAD CROSSED THE BARRIER, AND NOW THERE WAS NO turning back. Once I had kissed Dave it was impossible to stop kissing him. And as long as I was kissing him, it was a sign to him that I was fair game, and he increased his pursuit.

As the days went by we developed a very pleasant relationship. Dave went out of his way to spend every free moment with me—I would look up, and, unexpectedly, he would be there, his eyes glowing with so much love that my heart couldn't help but soar. Dave was always there to dance with me at night, hold my hand and put his arm around me and kiss me. We had long conversations about our lives, our families, and our aspirations, and I found that Dave had many of the qualities I had always wanted Lenny to have. He had a wonderful, stable family life, living with both his parents in a large private home in the suburbs of Boston; he did well in school; he had a great future as a lawyer in store for him. And he respected my wishes to keep our physical relationship limited to kissing, even though I knew he wanted more.

My relationship with Dave was so much simpler than my relationship with Lenny. Being with Lenny was something like a ride on a roller coaster; with him I had experienced the ultimate highs, but also the lowest lows. I had always tried to change what was wrong with Lenny, to fix him and get him to do things I thought were right, and there were always conflicts and tension between us. With Dave there was nothing I felt compelled to change; as a result, we had no conflicts, and our relationship was on easy, level ground. Dave was always full of compliments, telling me how good I looked, how beautiful my eyes were, how he thought the things I said were clever and brilliant, how wonderful it was to find a girl who had deep feelings and cared about other people and wasn't out to see how much a boy could do for her. I loved the feeling of being wanted and appreciated.

I felt great when I was with Dave, but I didn't feel great when I thought of Lenny. Dave was good to me, and I liked him more and more each day, but Lenny was the one I loved and had committed myself to. But if I really loved Lenny as much as I thought I did, how could I be getting so involved with Dave? Was it possible to love two boys at once? It was all very confusing, and I was torn by guilt.

The first time Lenny called me after that night with Dave I could hardly bring myself to speak to him.

"Hi, sweetheart. Boy, have I missed hearing your voice. I'm so miserable here without you. The only thing that keeps me going is the thought of being with you again," he said.

His words only served to increase my guilt feelings. "Oh—I—uh—I miss you, too," I managed to say.

"You sound strange, Linda. Is something wrong?"

"No. Uh, nothing's wrong."

"Is something going on I need to know about? Like with that guy who's after you, Dave?"

"No, no. Nothing! I mean we're just very friendly and all that."

"Well, make sure that weasel understands that you're mine, and he's not to get too friendly."

"He understands, he understands. He even told me he feels like 'just friends' is now his name."

Lenny didn't laugh, but he did get off the topic of Dave. I breathed a sigh of relief. I was a person who liked to be open and honest. I hated to lie and to deceive anyone, especially Lenny, but at this point, what else could I do? Telling him about the physical contact between me and Dave could only serve to hurt Lenny. It didn't mean anything anyway. A summer away in the country like this was a fantasy. It was easy to become enchanted by the magic and the romance. Once the summer was over and Dave went back to Boston and I went back to New York and had to deal with the realities of everyday life again, it would be over. I would be back to the Linda I knew, loving Lenny and only Lenny.

My guilt feelings worsened with my next conversation with Lenny. That's when he told me he had been so sick with stomach pains and high fever that he had spent most of the week in sick bay instead of going to classes. Lenny had gone through a period of being sick a lot when he was in boot camp that had really worried me, but he had seemed fine recently. The fact that he was sick again with the same symptoms he had had before was very upsetting.

"Oh, Lenny, that's awful! Are you okay now?"

"I seem okay. But I'm afraid it could happen again, and I don't trust the navy doctors—they still haven't been able to find out why I keep getting sick. Not only that, but this illness put me so far behind in my classwork, I'm going to have to work like crazy to catch up. I don't know how I'm going to do it."

"You'll do it, Lenny. I know you can." I tried to encourage him. I felt terrible that Lenny was having such a hard time of it while I was enjoying myself here in the country. The fooling around with Dave might not mean anything, but I knew that if Lenny found out about it, he would be really hurt and upset nonetheless. I resolved to end this thing with Dave right away, before it had a chance to do any damage.

For two days I kept out of his way and avoided seeing him, hibernating in my room with the excuse that I didn't feel well and needed rest. But I couldn't keep that up for long. I hated staying by myself in my room, with nothing but a novel to keep me company. And I could see by the look on Dave's face when I passed him at the pool without stopping for a few friendly words, as I did ordinarily, that he was hurt and confused by my actions. This made me feel lousy as well. It seemed that no matter which course of action I took I was going to wind up hurting somebody.

Roz told me I was being silly, and that I should be thrilled to have two boys who wanted me so much. I was far from thrilled. I was miserable.

The next night was Saturday, and as was typical for

Saturday nights at the Grandview, the kids had planned something special. This week it was a campfire. We would barbecue hot dogs and toast marshmallows and sing songs and tell ghost stories. I had really been looking forward to the campfire, but now that I was trying to avoid Dave, I decided it would be better if I didn't go.

"Not go? Why on earth not?" demanded Roz when I told her my decision Saturday afternoon. We were out in the playground pushing some kids on the swings.

"Because if I go, something is bound to happen with Dave. I can't stand the guilt, Roz. The more that goes on with Dave, the guiltier I feel because I know I'm hurting Lenny. As long as I'm committed to him I have no business fooling around with Dave or anyone else. What I'm doing is totally wrong!"

"Says who?" Roz demanded.

"Says me. I keep having these arguments with myself. Part of me tells me it's right to be loyal to Lenny. The other part of me longs to be with Dave."

"You poor thing. Do you know that what you're describing is a classic conflict between head and heart?"

"Conflict between head and heart? What are you talking about, Roz?"

"Well, I once read this philosophical article that claimed people are made up of three parts: mind or head, heart, and body. Everything goes along great as long as these three parts want the same thing, but unfortunately, it rarely works that way. It's not working that way in your case right now. Your head is telling you you should be loyal to Lenny, but your

heart and body are crying out for Dave. The result—
the conflict you are feeling." Roz looked very proud of
herself for having analyzed my situation so cleverly.

"That sounds great, Roz. Except for one thing. It's
Lenny my heart really belongs to. I've loved him for
three years, remember?"

"Love, love, love! Linda's in love!" sang out Jody,
this spoiled little kid I was pushing on the swing. That
did it for me. The last thing I needed was to have my
business spread all over the hotel by some four-year-
old brat.

"Okay, Jody, swinging time is over now." I stopped
the swing and lifted her out. "Go play in the sandbox." I quieted her protests. "Roz and I have to get
ready for your art project."

Roz followed my lead and took her kid out of the
swing as well. As we set up the art materials on the
table we could continue our conversation without
being overheard.

"This is the way I look at it," said Roz. "You care
for Dave enough that your heart wants to have some
sort of relationship with him, but your head tells you
that to do so would be a betrayal of Lenny. Result—
you feel guilty and don't know what to do."

"That's right, I don't." I sighed as I set up jars of
finger paint on the picnic table where we did our
outdoor crafts. "What do you think I should do?"

"Only you can decide that. But I'll tell you one
thing—if you really want to have Dave, you shouldn't
feel guilty about it, because it's not wrong; what would
be wrong would be to give him up for Lenny's sake.
You know it's my personal opinion that you shouldn't
be tied down to any boy, but we're not talking about
what I want. You're the one who has to listen to what

your head, heart, and body are telling you, and make your decision based on that."

"I want to finger-paint first!" Jody came running up to the table and demanded. The other kids followed her lead and were soon swarming over the picnic table, clamoring to paint. I saw my opportunity for a private conversation with Roz had ended. But she had already told me what I needed to hear. It was up to me to examine my heart and my head and see if I could get them together.

That afternoon, before I could make up my mind whether or not to go to the campfire, I received an unexpected call from Lenny.

"I had to call and tell you the news, Linda! I'm getting out of the navy! They're letting me out!"

"Out of the navy! But how? When? Why?"

"They're giving me a discharge for medical reasons. After I spoke to you I had another episode of stomach pain and fever. The doctors gave me all sorts of tests for every major disease you can think of, and I don't have any of them. They sent me to a therapist, but he couldn't find any psychological reason for my illness either. Then everyone involved had a conference and came to the only logical conclusion. As long as I keep getting sick, the navy can't help me, and I can't be of use to the navy. That's why they're letting me go. It'll take a few weeks for the paperwork and all, but from what they tell me, I should be getting home by the end of the summer. Won't that be wonderful?"

"I guess," I said hesitantly.

He picked right up on my hesitation. "What's the matter, Linda? We can be together again—I thought you'd be as happy about that as I am."

"I *am* happy about that, but one thing bothers me. All the reasons that you joined the navy in the first place—because you couldn't get along living with your mother at home, because you needed schooling so you could get a decent job, because you wanted to get away from the bad influences in the neighborhood, like your friends who were into gambling and staying out all night—none of that's changed. What's going to have gotten better when you come back home again?"

"I've changed," he said firmly. "I've done a lot of growing up since I joined the navy seven months ago. I've gotten through basic training successfully and learned to be responsible for myself and to take adverse conditions like being sick and having to do backbreaking work. I'm aware of how important it is for me to get on the right path once I get home, and I'm going to do it, Linda. Trust me, that's all. Things will work out; I know they will."

"I think they will, too, Lenny. It's just—it's so hard being separated from you like this."

"But that's all coming to an end soon. Be a little patient and—"

I heard a click, and then a dial tone letting me know we had been cut off. I waited by the phone, hoping Lenny would call me back again, but he didn't.

What Lenny had told me did nothing to resolve the conflict within me. Instead of being overjoyed by his news, I was even further confused. As much as I loved Lenny, the existence he had been leading before he joined the navy had created nothing but trouble. I wasn't sure that he had been in the navy long enough to straighten out, especially since he would be leaving before having a chance to finish his school program. I didn't want to go back to the way things were before, when we were having so many fights about the fact that he was doing nothing to better his life and our future together.

I leaned up against the phone booth, deep in thought, my head resting in my hands.

"Life couldn't be that terrible." The voice broke my concentration. I whirled around, and it was Dave. Here I was, face to face with him, unable to avoid him any longer.

"I just got off the phone with Lenny. He's getting a discharge, coming home from the navy."

"Oh." You could see Dave turn pale, even under his summer tan. "And when will that be?"

"Probably not till the end of the summer."

"Good. Then it makes absolutely no difference to us, anyhow." He bent to kiss me, but I pushed him away.

"Dave! This is all happening too fast for me! I don't know if I can handle it!"

"There's nothing to handle, Linda. Don't make such a big deal over everything; relax and let nature take its course. I've got to go meet Perry now. I'll see you tonight at the campfire."

"I'm not sure if I'm go—" Before I could finish my statement Dave was gone. And I still didn't know what was right for me to do.

The more I thought about my situation, the more I felt the right thing to do would be to end it with Dave before we became further involved. I decided to go to the campfire and find an opportunity to talk to him and explain the reasons for my decision.

The campfire started out to be great fun. All the kids gathered the wood, built the fire, and sat around in one big group as we cooked and ate our food, told our stories, and sang our songs. Then the temperature dropped, and to keep warm we wrapped ourselves in blankets and huddled around the fire.

That's when people began pairing off, kissing and making out under the blankets. That's when I realized this was not going to be a good place to break anything to Dave.

I had told Dave before we came to the campfire that I had a lot of thinking to do, and I would appreciate it if he would limit our physical contact to hand-holding. So far, he had gone along with my wishes, although I could tell by the tenseness in his body that he was far from happy with the situation.

"Mel and I are going back to the room to warm up," Roz came over to me and said with a wink. I got her message. She wanted a block of time alone with Mel.

"Okay. I won't be back till late," I told her, although I knew this would increase the pressure on me with Dave.

Once Roz and Mel left, Perry and Alice, the girl he was with, left, too. A few at a time, other couples drifted off on their own, until Dave and I were the only ones remaining at the campfire.

Under the blanket we sat, side by side, holding hands and watching the fire. That is, I was watching the fire; I could sense that Dave was watching me. I struggled to find the right words with which to tell him that we had to stop all physical contact before further damage was done.

I took a deep breath and came out with it. "Dave, we can't go on like this. The summer will be over, and someone's going to wind up getting hurt," I began. I turned to him, and that's when I saw, in the light of the campfire, the anguish and longing etched into his face.

His grip tightened on my hand. "I can't worry about what might happen when the summer is over, Linda. I can't look into the future and predict what is going to be. This moment, now, is all I have, and all that matters to me. And the only thing I can tell you is that I've come to love you, Linda. And I want you more than I've wanted anything in my life. I love you, I really do!"

I looked into his eyes, brimming with unshed tears, and I saw that he meant what he had said. He really believed he loved me and that this moment was all he had. How could I be so cruel as to turn him away?

His face drew closer, and I found myself unable to protest. His lips crushed mine in a kiss so intense and passionate I could feel all his pent-up longing. I found myself responding to his urgency and kissing him back.

That's when I realized that I was caught up in a flow of events that I was powerless to control. Lenny would get out of the navy, he would be furious about Dave, and our love might or might not be strong enough to get over it. My relationship with Dave might or might not stand the test of time and separation once we left the country and went back home. I had no idea in which direction the future might lead me.

But all I could do was go with the flow.

Chapter

Five

DAVE LOVED ME; I SAW IT IN THE WAY HE LOOKED AT ME, in every word he spoke and gesture he made. Dave loved me, and sometimes I felt very powerful emotional responses toward him, but did that mean I loved him, too? For a long time I had thought I knew what love was; with Lenny there had been no question in my mind. But if what I felt for Lenny was real love, how could I explain the times when I thought I felt the same way toward Dave? Was it possible to love two people at once, or were my confused feelings evidence that I really loved neither?

I had the questions, but I didn't have the answers. I only knew that as long as I didn't think about Lenny, the summer was one of the best in my life. The beautiful mountains and sunsets, the sun-drenched heat of the days and the star-spangled cool of the nights wove a magically romantic spell I had no power to resist.

I went with the flow, and by mid-August events had led to the gradual strengthening of my relationship with Dave. Once I had stopped fighting the inevitable, we were together all the time. On rainy days he came to stay with me in the kiddy camp building, or we would sit together watching the movies he showed in the rec hall. On sunny days I saw him at the pool and on the grounds. And nights, those magical, romantic nights, we danced together and walked and talked and made out to our hearts' content.

"Linda, I've been thinking," he began quite innocently one night when we were sitting together in our spot by the pool. "You haven't even started college yet; you're not locked into Barnard in any way. Why don't you put in an application at U. Mass.? It would be so great if we could go to the same school."

I immediately felt the knot in my stomach that appeared there whenever I was reminded that someday I was going to have to make a choice between Lenny and Dave. "That's really impossible, Dave. My parents couldn't afford to send me to an out-of-state school. The only reason I'm going to Barnard is because I got good financial aid and I'm living at home to save costs."

"Oh." His face fell. He thought for a moment and then brightened. "Well, my parents are already paying top dollar for my education. I bet I could find somewhere in New York City comparable in cost to U. Mass. and transfer there. My parents give me almost everything I want. I'm sure I could convince them to go along with this, too."

I blinked, not sure I had heard him correctly. "Dave, are you serious? You've had two years at U. Mass.; you told me yourself how great the campus was and how much you loved the school. Why would you want to transfer to the city?"

He gazed into my eyes with an intensity that was frightening. "Because I love you, Linda. Because I can't stand the thought of being without you when the summer's over. Say the word and I'll start the transfer process tomorrow!"

I was not ready to handle this. "Oh, Dave, I wouldn't think of having you change schools at this point. Try to understand—I have to see Lenny before I can make any decisions, to find out how I really feel about him and how this thing between you and me was able to happen. Let's keep things the way they are for now, and we can discuss it again after the first term of college."

Dave was not happy with my answer, but for the time being he accepted it. He had no choice but to accept the way I felt in every aspect of our relationship. His position with me was too uncertain for him to try to force his will. Dave knew perfectly well that as much as I cared for him, I had not yet made up my mind to choose him over Lenny.

As for my relationship with Lenny, it seemed to be getting worse in inverse proportion to the way things were going with Dave. Our letters and phone calls were filled with arguments about what would be the best thing for him to do once he left the navy. He wanted to find a job and take some courses at night. I thought it would make more sense for him to concentrate on schooling so he could get a better job someday, and to work only enough to get some spending money. Whenever we discussed the subject we would wind up feeling tense and angry.

On top of our heated arguments on this sensitive

LOVING TWO IS HARD TO DO

issue, Lenny never spoke to me without making some mention of Dave. Having to tell Lenny that Dave was not important to me when this was no longer the truth set my nerves on edge, and I was such a terrible liar that it was obvious that Lenny didn't believe me. Instead of looking forward to his phone calls, I came to dread them. My greatest fear was that Lenny would get his discharge before the summer was over and decide to come up to the country.

On August 17, at precisely five o'clock, came the call I had dreaded most. "It's happened, Linda. Finally! My papers arrived today. Two more days and I'll be officially discharged from the navy, a free man!"

"That's—uh—that's great, Lenny!" My heart was pounding with fear. "What are you going to do, go straight to New York?"

"That's my first destination. Then I was thinking of taking a little vacation. Somewhere nice and restful, like the White Mountains of New Hampshire!"

I didn't know what to say. How could I tell my boyfriend of three years that it would be disastrous for him to come up and see me when that had been the main thing he had been looking forward to for so long? "Well, uh—well, Lenny, I'm not sure that would be such a good idea. Not that I'm not eager to see you, or anything, but it could cause problems up here."

"Problems? What sort of problems?"

"Well, I—uh—er, the owners don't like the staff to bring friends here. They think that kind of thing interferes with doing our jobs properly. And I really won't have much time to spend with you. I'm busy with the kids all day long. Besides, you should be devoting your attention to getting your act together there in the city. And it's not that long before the

43

summer will be over, and I'll be back home again. It's better to wait until then."

"Are you kidding, Linda? None of those reasons are worth staying away from you one day longer than I have to. Unless—unless—"

"Unless what?"

"Unless there's something going on there you haven't told me about to keep me away. Like with that Dave. That's it, isn't it, Linda? You don't want me to come up and spoil your thing with him!"

"No! No, that's not the case at all, Lenny. You don't understand!" Desperately, I tried to put aside his suspicions. "You'd have to see the routine here to know how hard it is to have visitors. It would be too much for me. That's why I don't want you to come!"

I heard him suck in his breath, and then there was a moment of silence. When he finally did begin to speak his voice held a mixture of anger and pain. "Well, now you said it—you don't want me to come. I never thought I'd live to hear those words from your mouth, Linda. Not from you. Well, I'll think about those words good and hard when I'm getting out of the navy and going back to the city. I'll think about the welcome home I got from you and wonder what I did to deserve it. But don't rest too easily, Linda, because you never know. At any moment, when you least expect it, I could turn up before your very eyes!"

He hung up before I could say anything else. I was left feeling so awful, I was tempted to call the navy to try to speak to him some more. But I had no idea of how and where to call to try to find him, and talking to him would probably make matters even worse.

I decided to wait until Lenny got home before trying to contact him. In the meantime I hoped that he would come to his senses and decide not to visit New Hampshire after all.

If Lenny was to get his discharge on August 19 and go to the city first, the soonest he could get up to New Hampshire was August 20. I didn't really think he would come after the conversation we had had, but I wasn't sure.

All day on the twentieth I found myself going absolutely crazy thinking about it. To relieve the tension I told the kids in my camp group that a friend of mine, named Lenny, might be coming on the bus that night. We made a game of going to the bus stop to see who would be first to spot the bus, and then who would guess who Lenny might be.

The bus was due at seven-fifteen, right before we brought the kids back to the dining room to meet their parents. Roz and I sat the kids on the front lawn on top of a hill, where we had a good view of the bus stop, and sang songs with them to pass the time. We were in the middle of "The Wheels on the Bus Go Round and Round" when Dave made his appearance.

"I've been looking all over for you, Linda, but you were in none of the places you usually take the kids. What are you doing here?"

"We're waiting for the bus to see if Lenny's on it!" Jody piped up. For a little girl, she certainly had a big mouth.

"What does she mean, if Lenny's on it?" Dave looked at me questioningly.

"Oh, it's a game we're playing," I told him nervously. "I really don't think Lenny will be on the bus after I made it clear I didn't want him to come. But, of course, with him you never know!"

"He'd better not be." Dave had a glum look on his face as he stood by our group.

The bus was late, and we were gathering up the kids to take them to the dining room when we heard the sound of a vehicle approaching.

"The bus! The bus! I see the bus!" Jody called out. "And I bet that's Lenny getting off now! Am I right, Linda? Did I win for spotting him first?"

"You sure did," Roz answered for me, for I couldn't say a word. I stood there as if frozen to the spot, staring at the apparition of Lenny emerging from the bus and intruding on my neat little world of the country where he didn't belong. He looked at me and then at Dave, and then back at me again, and I knew that whatever happened, nothing would ever be the same again between us.

It was Roz who broke the ice. "Hi, Lenny! Welcome to the Grandview Hotel! I'm sure you and Linda have a lot to talk about, so I'll take the kids back to the dining room now. See you later."

"Okay, later." Lenny barely acknowledged her. He turned to me. "Well, Linda. Is this the kind of greeting you give me after not seeing me for two months?"

The hurt in his voice got through to me and shook me back to reality. "Oh, Lenny, I'm sorry, I was just so shocked to see you—I didn't really think you would come!" I went over to give him a hug.

"Nothing would keep me from you, Linda— nothing!" He wrapped his arms around me and kissed me right there. I clung to him, and that's when I noticed how thin he was. I could feel the bones right through his T-shirt. He must have lost at least ten pounds since I had last seen him!

46

I pulled back from him and looked him over. His face was thin and drawn and haggard, and his color was pale. "Oh, Lenny, what happened? You look as if you've been much sicker than you've let me know."

"I have," he said. "But that's not important now. What matters is that I'm here with you."

I hugged him again, and then I looked up and saw Dave. For a moment I had forgotten all about him, but there he was, still standing on the spot where he had been when the bus arrived, and looking at us with an expression of distaste.

I don't know what I would have done then if Roz hadn't returned. She took one look at our little scene and decided to take charge of it. "Well, I think we all know each other, except for Dave and Lenny. How about if you two be adult and civilized about everything, shake hands, and start out as friends?"

"Okay with me." Dave approached Lenny and cautiously extended his hand. "I'm Dave Balen. I can't say that I'm glad to meet you, but Roz is right. We might as well be adult and civilized."

Lenny loosened his grip on me, and for a moment I actually thought he might shake Dave's hand. He didn't. "Adult and civilized? That's easy for you to say, since I haven't been working all summer to steal your girl away from you, you dirty, sneaking, low-down—"

Lenny came out with a string of curse words that made me want to sink right into the ground and disappear. I saw Dave's face go red with anger, and he clenched his extended hand into a fist.

"No, Dave, don't!" I stepped in front of him before he could hit Lenny. "We don't want any fighting! We could both lose our jobs, and someone could get hurt!"

"That someone is going to be him!" Lenny put his fists up and moved in closer to Dave. "I'll turn this stumpy little punk into mincemeat!"

"Lenny, please!" I turned to him and begged. "Just give me one minute to talk to Dave, and then I'll spend the rest of the evening with you, I promise!"

For a moment it looked as if Lenny was too angry to back off, but then he did. "One minute," he said warningly, then he went over to talk to Roz.

I motioned to Dave to come over and talk to me behind a tree. He gave Lenny one last glare, then followed me.

"I should have killed him!" Dave pounded his fist into his palm. "Who does he think he is, coming up here and taking over? You're not married to the guy! He doesn't own you!"

"No, but I do owe him a lot for all the years we've been together," I said. I felt awful, torn in two directions, not knowing which way to turn. I didn't want to hurt either of them, but there was no way we were going to get out of this situation without someone's being hurt. "Please try to understand, Dave. You can't pay any attention to the awful things Lenny said—it's only because he's so hurt and angry. He came all the way up here to see me, and I've got to spend this time with him—it's the only way to find out how I really feel about both of you. You've got to be big enough to back off and leave us alone together. Do it for me, Dave. Please!"

Dave looked at me, and I could see how hard this was for him. He clasped me briefly to his chest. "Okay," he said, and his voice cracked with emotion.

"I'll leave you alone with him until tomorrow." Then he let go and walked away.

It was so strange being with Lenny in all the places that, until now, I had gone to only with Dave. We went to get Lenny something to eat at Sam's Café and sat at a table by ourselves. I was uncomfortably aware of the looks I was getting from the group of kids who sat at our usual table, kids who were accustomed to having me there with them and with Dave. I couldn't wait to get out of Sam's and go sit out by the pool, where Lenny and I could at least be alone.

But being alone with Lenny was not any easier. Lenny was brutal with me, demanding to know exactly what had been going on between Dave and me all summer and not letting up his questioning until he was satisfied I had told him every detail. I told him that I had fully intended for Dave and me to be "just friends," but things had gotten out of control and developed to the point where obviously we were a great deal more. It was especially painful to tell Lenny about the night Dave and I had first kissed, but I swore to him our physical relationship had gone no further than that.

I don't know if Lenny believed me or if it even mattered whether he did. The hurt he was feeling from my betrayal of him was horrible to see.

His eyes grew misty, and his voice cracked when he spoke. "You have no idea how sick I've been, Linda—how hard it's been for me to get through these last few months in the navy. And all the time the thing that kept me going was the thought of you, loyal and waiting for me. You were like the vision of an angel to me; I had you up on a pedestal. And now that vision is shattered—it's as if you shot me in my heart! How could you do this to me, Linda? How could you?"

Nothing he could have said would have made me feel worse. Hot tears rushed to and spilled out of my eyes. "Oh, Lenny, I'm so sorry!" I sobbed. "I didn't want to do anything to hurt you—this thing with Dave was not something I was looking for or wanted to occur. I kept fighting what was happening, but after a while it became much too strong to fight. I thought I loved you—I really did! I had no idea I could feel anything for any other boy. I had no idea!"

I put my hand on his shoulder, and he turned back to face me. He saw my tears and took me in his arms. "I still love you, Linda. I don't know why, but I do."

He kissed me with tremendous passion, and I kissed him back, my heart aching for having caused him so much pain. We made out for a while, both of us trying to recapture what we had once had together, but it was not like it used to be. In the past it had always felt right to be making love because I had been so sure of my feelings for Lenny, but this was no longer the case. Now I felt strangely detached from him. My body was going through the motions, but my head and heart weren't in it.

Lenny must have sensed my detachment, because he pulled away from me. "It's not working, is it? That connection we always had between us has been severed. You don't love me anymore, do you?"

I felt awful to hear him express it that way. I didn't want to hurt him further, but it was probably better to be honest than to try to pretend. "I don't know, Lenny, I just don't know. I still care for you, I really do! But I can't truthfully swear that I still love you, because I don't know if I could feel the way I do about

Dave at the same time. I'm so confused—it's so hard—I just don't know what to do!"

"What to do? The choice is clear to me, Linda. You can still have me if you want me, but you're going to have to end it with Dave. You can't be my girl and carry on with him at the same time!"

"Your girl!" I repeated the words, and suddenly the direction I had to take became clear to me. "Oh, no, Lenny, it can no longer be that way. I'm too young; I'm too unsure of what it is I really want. I'll be starting college this year, meeting lots of new people, having new opportunities. This is a time in my life when I need to be free—free to get to know others and to get to know myself as well. As much as we've been through together and as much as I've loved you, I don't want to be tied down to you. I don't want to be tied to Dave either, for that matter. I'm willing to see you whenever you want to see me, but it has to be on my terms. At this point I have to have the freedom to date without having to answer to you or anyone else!"

"You can't mean that, Linda! Not when I love you so much!" He stared at me, his eyes full of anguish, and for a moment I was tempted to back down from my stance. But something inside of me knew that the decision was right for me.

We stayed up half the night, talking about it over and over, and Lenny used all his tremendous powers of persuasion to make me see things differently. I didn't waver. I knew my freedom was something I had to have, even if it meant losing Lenny. He could accept our relationship under these terms, or he could break up with me. It was up to him.

Chapter

Six

NOTHING I SAID TO LENNY WOULD CONVINCE HIM THAT the route I had decided to take—to date him and others, too—was the right one. "It might have worked once for us, Linda, but not now," he told me. "There was too much between us to go backward—I was seriously thinking of marrying you. If you want Dave and your freedom to mess around, that's it for us. We're through."

I begged him to reconsider, telling him that if he could agree to give me the freedom I needed for now, there was a good chance it would someday work out for us, but he refused to accept a relationship like that. It was all or nothing with Lenny, and since I couldn't give him what he wanted, he would give me nothing. Filled with anger and resentment, he left for the city without even kissing me goodbye.

I felt awful about what had happened. I hadn't wanted to end my relationship with Lenny, certainly not with all this hostility and pain.

Dave was right there to comfort me. That night we sat by the pool discussing the situation. I told him how I had been depressed all day over what had happened with Lenny, blaming myself for having hurt him so much.

He put his arm around me and stroked my hair with great tenderness. "Don't be so hard on yourself, Linda. Once you decided you didn't want to go steady with Lenny anymore, you couldn't really have done much differently. Besides, you really are better off without him. This had to happen, or you would wind up regretting it later. You may not realize it now, but Lenny actually did you a favor by breaking up with you. Of course, he did *me* a great favor, too!"

Dave grinned broadly, and I couldn't help laughing. I thought about what he said and began to feel better. "You're right, Dave. This is something that had to happen to me at this point in my life. After all, I've been romantically involved with Lenny ever since I was old enough to start dating. My experience with other boys is practically nonexistent, and I have no idea of what the dating scene is like. I need to find out about things like that before I commit myself to settling down with anyone."

"Well, don't get so carried away with this 'experience' stuff that you fail to recognize a good thing when it's right in front of your nose," Dave said. "Like me, for example. There's nothing wrong with settling down with me!"

"Dave! You can't be serious! I just finished telling you that I couldn't go along with Lenny's demands on me because I needed to have some freedom. I thought you understood my feelings."

Linda Lewis

"I do, I do—you're free to go out with whomever you want," Dave said quickly. "But you can't blame a guy for hoping, can you? I've had plenty of experience with other girls, and I can tell you, none of it means anything until you find the one you love. But I'll be patient. I don't think it's going to take you long to get tired of the dating scene, and when you do, I want to be right there waiting to make you my own."

"That's fine, Dave, as long as you accept my feelings. This thing I've gone through with Lenny has left me very confused. You have to give me some time to learn what it is I really want."

About a week after Lenny's visit I received a letter that helped me feel better about what I had done. It was from Fran Zaro, who was my other best friend in the city. Like Roz, Fran had once been going steady but was now out there dating as many boys as she possibly could. Also like Roz, Fran had been trying to convince me for a long time to do the same. She was overjoyed to find out I had finally untied myself from Lenny.

Dear Linda,

I was absolutely thrilled to get your letter saying you had broken up with Lenny. Finally, at age seventeen, you are opening yourself up to seeing what life has to offer you. I'm firmly convinced that it's impossible to make a decision as to what boy you eventually want to have a permanent relationship with unless you have experience with lots of different boys. Believe me, you're doing the right thing by insisting on your freedom and only "no strings attached" relationships for now,

54

and you shouldn't feel guilty about it. Your relationship with Lenny would never work out as long as you still had unresolved questions in your mind about whether it was what you really wanted, and now you'll have the opportunity to find out.

Fran went on to say that she had selfish reasons for being glad that I was now a free agent as well. Roz was going away in September to the State University at Buffalo, so Fran was glad to have me available to go with her to parties and places where we could meet new boys.

Meeting new boys. It made my head swim to think of it. Barnard girls got to take classes with boys from Columbia University, some of the brightest boys in the country. Once school started, and there were all sorts of college parties and activities going on, I should have no trouble meeting boys to go out with. There would be boys from my neighborhood who might ask me out once they knew I was available. I might meet someone through Fran or some of my other friends. Maybe once Lenny had calmed down, he would decide he was willing to do some casual dating. And of course, there would be Dave. Massachusetts was close enough for us to be able to see each other regularly if things kept going the way they had been.

Without Lenny as an obstacle between us, my feelings for Dave grew stronger during those last days of August. Dave was always good to me, always considerate, always pleasant. He was the boyfriend I had always fantasized—a clean-cut, successful college boy, loving, handsome, with a wonderful career ahead of him. We never fought about anything. I was beginning to think that Dave was absolutely perfect when the problem with Roz arose.

It started in small ways. I became aware of a strange hostility whenever Roz and Dave were together. They would throw little nasty remarks at each other or exchange dirty looks. I didn't understand what was going on between them. But there was one thing I did understand—that we all lived too close together for my best friend not to be getting along with my boyfriend.

I spoke to Roz about this one afternoon when we were alone in our room. "What's been going on between you and Dave, Roz? Recently I've been getting the distinct feeling that you don't like him."

Roz sank back on her bed and sighed. "I have nothing specific against Dave, Linda, except for his attitude. Ever since Lenny left, Dave acts as if you're his personal property and no one else matters. I get the feeling he resents me for being your friend and demanding some of your time and attention. He's so selfish that he wants you all to himself."

"But Roz," I protested, "Dave loves me. It's natural for him to want to be around me in the short time we have left in the summer."

"Well, that doesn't mean he has to treat me like I'm some sort of dirt pile who's in his way," Roz said hotly.

I tried to convince Roz that all this was in her head and Dave didn't resent her, but nothing I said would change her opinion. My next step was to approach Dave and tell him how Roz felt.

"That's all a bunch of bull!" he insisted. "If you ask

me, the problem is that Roz is jealous because she sees I care for you much more than Mel will ever care for her. That's why she resents having me around."

Nothing I said seemed to change Dave's opinion either. It was becoming very uncomfortable to be around Roz and Dave together, and I didn't know what to do about it.

Everything came to a head one night after dinner. Roz and I ate our dinner with the kids in our group, and most of the rest of the hotel staff ate at that time as well. Dave had developed the habit of eating his meal as quickly as possible, then bringing his chair over to our table to sit with me until my kids were finished eating. I always looked forward to that little extra time with Dave.

I knew Roz really wasn't wild about this habit, but she had never said anything about it until the end of the summer when the tensions between her and Dave were at their height. The problem started with Stacey Marshall, a camper who had arrived at the Grandview for the last week of the season. Stacey was a cute, bright little girl of five with one major liability—a mother who was ridiculously overprotective. All Stacey's first day, Mrs. Marshall hung around kiddy camp, not wanting to let her precious daughter out of her sight. Roz and I finally had to tell Mrs. Marshall that she was disrupting our group and she would have to decide whether to leave Stacey with us or to take her out of camp.

"Okay, I'll leave her with you," Mrs. Marshall reluctantly agreed when she saw how much fun Stacey was having. "But Stacey's a picky eater. I have to be there at mealtime to make sure she's eating properly."

I was sure that Stacey would eat a lot better if her

mother wasn't always hovering around, but I didn't want to argue. Roz and I told Mrs. Marshall she could sit with us in the dining room.

That was a big mistake. Not only did Mrs. Marshall fuss about what Stacey was eating, but she thought it was her business what the other kids ate as well. And then she decided it was her business that Dave was coming to sit at our table.

"You don't belong here," she said to him bluntly. "You're not a counselor. All you do is distract the girls' attention so they can't watch the kids properly."

By that time I had had about all I could take of this busybody's interference, and I decided to tell her so. "Dave isn't distracting anyone, Mrs. Marshall." I struggled to keep my voice sounding polite. "In fact, there are times he actually helps us with the kids."

Mrs. Marshall seemed to accept my explanation, but Roz didn't let the matter rest. "Actually, Mrs. Marshall is absolutely right, Dave. You really don't belong at our table." She smiled sweetly when she said this, but I knew perfectly well she was trying to get at Dave. Fortunately, Dave laughed this off as if it were just a joke.

It wasn't until later, when Mrs. Marshall left us to have her own dinner, that Roz and Dave had the chance to express their true feelings. Dave followed us down to the playground, grabbed Roz by her shirt, and pinned her up against the climbing bars.

"What are you trying to do, Roz? Stir up trouble by telling that parent I don't belong at your table?" he demanded.

"Well, it so happens you don't, Dave Balen." Roz shoved him away from her. "To tell you the truth, I'm sick of seeing your ugly face appear whenever I'm with Linda."

"Ugly face! You wish you looked as good as I do! Then maybe you could attract some boy who wasn't two-timing you behind your back!" Dave's face was flushed as he said this. I had never seen him so angry before, and it was frightening. So were the words he had uttered. Who was two-timing Roz behind her back?

Roz obviously had no idea what he was talking about. Her face grew absolutely white, and her voice got so low I could barely hear it as she demanded to know exactly what Dave meant by that remark.

It was with a sadistic sense of delight that Dave told her. He had overheard Mel bragging about how, on the nights he told Roz he was too tired to see her and had to catch up on his sleep, he was actually seeing Cheryl, a waitress at the Mountaindale, the hotel across the street.

I have to hand it to Roz. She didn't give Dave the satisfaction of seeing how devastated she was by this news. It wasn't until late that night, when we were alone in our room, that I heard her sobbing into her pillow. She told me she had confronted Mel, and he had admitted that what Dave had said was true. He couldn't understand why she was so upset over it. He was out to have as good a time as possible for the summer, and he had given Roz plenty of pleasure along the way.

"I was nothing but a passing fling for him, Linda," she wailed. "Mel never cared for me, never cared for anything but what he wanted to do!"

"Well, if that's the case, it's a good thing you found

out about him before it was too late." I tried to comfort her. "The more you became involved with him, the worse your hurt would have been."

"That's not true, Linda!" She sat up abruptly in her bed. "I could have gotten through the summer blissfully unaware that Mel was two-timing me, and our relationship could have died a natural death when we got back to the city. I never would have had to deal with this at all if it wasn't for the cruelty of your boyfriend Dave. He's got a heart of ice to do something like this to me. I'm—I'm so un-unhappyyy!"

This last word turned into another wail, and she buried her head in the pillow once again. Nothing I could say that night would comfort her, and nothing could make her forgive Dave for the rest of the summer.

Dave insisted he had only told Roz about Mel because he thought she was better off knowing the truth, and I decided to believe him. This incident was unfortunate, but I didn't want it to ruin our last few days we had in the country. The summer—the wonderful, magical summer—was coming to an end all too soon, and I had no idea of what my return to the city would have in store for me.

I felt a surge of panic as I waited for the bus that would take Roz and me back to New York. It had been so easy to feel confident in New Hampshire when I knew Dave was always around to love and want me. It had been easy to feel confident in the past as long as I knew Lenny was always there for me. For the first time it hit me that I was faced with the stark reality of going back to the city and being on my own.

I clung tightly to Dave as the bus pulled up to the

Grandview. We kissed goodbye until the driver began to grumble that I was holding up his schedule, and I had no choice but to break away.

Dave ran up to my window to call out one last promise. "I'll be in to New York to see you the first chance I get!" He stood there, looking forlorn and all alone, waving to me until the bus was out of sight.

"Boy, what a disgusting exhibition of passion," Roz said glumly as she settled down next to me. "What is it about you, Linda, that makes these guys pledge their undying love for you, when all I got out of this summer was being two-timed by that dirty louse Mel?" Roz still hadn't gotten over the pain of rejection.

"Come on, Roz, don't feel so bad; Mel's not even worth it. Once you start school at Buffalo, I bet there will be loads of boys who will be interested in you, and you'll forget Mel even existed. As for my situation, don't be fooled into thinking it's so wonderful, either. Loving two boys is impossible to do for long, and I don't know what's going to happen with either Dave or Lenny. I haven't even heard from Lenny since he left the Grandview. For all I know, he'll never want to see me again."

"I doubt it," Roz said. "But truthfully, you'd be better off if he didn't. You know I never thought it was good for you to be so obsessed with Lenny, and this is a great opportunity for you to break the hold he has on you. But, of course, I don't think Dave is the right one for you either."

"Roz! You're just saying that because you're still sore at Dave for telling you about Mel."

"Not true," she insisted. "I saw plenty I didn't like about Dave before he pulled that nasty trick. I think he's a spoiled brat—he's had everything come too easily to him all his life. He's got this cold, unfeeling, stubborn, and cruel streak in him he likes to keep hidden, but when it comes out—forget it!"

"Don't you think you're exaggerating about Dave, Roz? He was always nice to me."

"Sure, because he went out of his way to be nice around you to make a good impression. I hope you'll never get to see that other side of him, Linda, but I still think you can do better. Find someone with Lenny's charm, personality, depth of feeling, and sense of humor combined with Dave's future, and you'll have it made!"

"Thanks a lot. I'll see if I can have someone made to order." I laughed and settled back for the long ride home.

As we got closer to the city I found myself thinking less about Dave and more about Lenny. It was very unlike him not to contact me, even though he had been angry at me when he left New Hampshire. I wondered if he had gotten home safely. I wondered if he had gotten his act together and was going forward with his life, or if he had gone back to the kind of self-destructive behavior that had upset me in the past, doing things like staying out all night bumming around with the boys, gambling on horse racing, and fighting with his mother. I wondered how he felt about me and if he still wanted me. I wondered how I would feel about him when I saw him again.

My heart hammered when I spotted the towers of the George Washington Bridge that spanned the Hudson River to connect the state of New Jersey with Washington Heights, the part of New York City where

I lived. The summer was over; it was really over. I was back home again, home to deal with reality.

I felt as if I were at a crossroads with many paths stretching out in front of me and no idea of which way to go. The direction I would take, the decisions I would make in the days ahead would affect me the rest of my life.

Chapter

Seven

IT DIDN'T TAKE ME LONG AFTER I HAD GOTTEN HOME TO have my first contact with Lenny. I managed to unpack my suitcase and fill my parents and brothers in on some of the things that had happened to me during the summer when I heard a familiar whistling coming from the courtyard. I ran to the window and saw Lenny standing there with his best friend, Sheldon Emory.

I wasn't sure if it was with happiness or with apprehension, but my heart leapt when I saw Lenny. He looked much better than he had in the country. It seemed he had put his weight back on.

"He's been hanging around here for the past two days, annoying us to find out when you were due back home," Ira told me.

"Isn't that boy ever going to leave you alone?" asked my mother, her normally pleasant face taking on a deep scowl. Both my parents had been very happy when I told them Lenny and I had broken up and that

I would be dating Dave and, hopefully, other boys as well. "Tell him to go away once and for all."

"Come on down, Linda. We need to talk," Lenny called up to me.

I looked from him to my parents and back down to him again. It would probably be best for me to say no to Lenny, to show him I was still firm in my decision.

But "no" wasn't what came out of my mouth. "I really owe it to Lenny to talk to him, even if it's just to let him know I haven't changed my mind," I explained to my parents. Before they could protest further, I was out the door and flying down the three flights of stairs that led to the street.

I stopped short when I reached the entrance to my apartment building. After all, I didn't want to give Lenny the impression that I was overly eager to see him. I only wanted to hear that he was okay and doing the right thing with his life. I opened the door that led to my courtyard and walked outside slowly.

Lenny and Sheldon were standing on my corner near the candy store where the kids in my crowd often hung out. They were leaning against a car and eating ice cream cones. My heart was pounding as I walked toward them. I had no idea how Lenny was going to react.

"Want some?" Lenny held his ice cream cone out to me as if nothing had changed between us. I noticed the cone was strawberry, my favorite, and not coffee, which was his.

"Okay, thanks." I took a bite, then handed him back the cone. As he took it his fingers brushed mine, and I felt a chill go through me. Darn it! He still affected me. I was going to have to try harder to steel myself against him. "So how've you been?" I asked.

"As well as anyone who's had his heart shattered could be," he answered with a bitter laugh. "Actually, Sheldon's been a big help. He lent me the money so the two of us could have a little vacation."

"Oh? Where did you go?"

"To a hotel up in the Catskill mountains," Sheldon replied. "My college was sponsoring a weekend there. We had a great time—golf, tennis, swimming, women. That brunette was the perfect prescription for healing a broken heart, wasn't she, Lenny?"

"Sure was." Lenny smiled pleasantly, and I felt an unwanted pang of anguish at the thought of him with this unidentified brunette. I told myself I was being silly. Lenny had every right to go out with whomever he wanted now that I had claimed my freedom.

"And what have you been doing since then?" I changed the topic. "Have you made up your mind about what school to go to?"

"Yes. No school at all, at least not for the time being. I'm going to look for a job until I know what direction to go in."

"But Lenny, that's exactly what you were doing before, and it didn't work then." I found myself arguing with him. "Why would you think it'll work now?"

"Because I have to have more money than I could make if I was in school all day. My mother's been especially nice to me since I got out of the navy, but I can already see the tension building between us when I ask her for money. She tells me to get it from my father, but he hardly ever comes around since they've been separated, and when he does, they fight so much I can't even get a word in. It probably won't be long before she begins fighting with me again. Under those circumstances, I can't count on being able to study. I've no choice but to get a job."

"Oh. That's too bad." The problems Lenny had at home were what had led him to get into trouble with school in the first place. I worried that he might get back into the same old rut that had been so bad for him before.

I worried. It took me a moment to remember that at this point there was no reason for me to worry about Lenny—he was no longer my boyfriend. But I still wanted to know that he was doing the right thing. "Have you started looking for jobs yet?"

"No. I need this time to unwind, gain some weight, and get my health and my strength back after all I've been through." He looked at me meaningfully.

I felt myself blushing. "Well, I hope you find what you want when you're ready."

He laughed so hard I thought he'd choke on his last bite of ice cream. "That is big of her, isn't it, Sheldon?" He poked Sheldon in the ribs, and Sheldon laughed along with him. "She carries on with that wormy weasel all summer, and now she comes home and tells me she hopes I find what I want!"

His sarcasm hurt. "Come on, Lenny. I do want the best for you. And I want us to always be friends, no matter what."

His laughter ceased. "Let's get one thing straight, Linda. Forget about friendship or any other kind of relationship with me as long as you're seeing that little puke. When's he coming here to New York, anyway?"

I swallowed. "I-I'm not sure. He said he'd call me tonight and try to see me before school starts."

"So he's dumb enough to think he can hold on to you from so far away? Well, you'd better tell him to be good and careful. Once he comes to the city he's in my territory, and anything can happen!" He turned from me and gestured to Sheldon. "Come on, Emory, let's get out of here and go where we can breathe some fresh air!"

Without giving me another glance he and Sheldon walked off down the street toward the park. He left me fuming. Here I had gone out of my way to try to be nice to Lenny, and all I had gotten were threats and insults. He made me so mad I could scream!

I was glad I had broken up with Lenny. I was. I was.

Dave came in to see me three days later. My parents agreed to let him stay at our house as long as he wanted to. They were eager to do everything they could to keep me away from Lenny.

It was as strange to be with Dave in the city as it was to have been with Lenny in the country. I kept getting this awful feeling that this was not where Dave belonged. I tried not to think those kind of thoughts but concentrated instead on all the things Dave and I were to do together.

We spent the weekend traveling around the city, visiting sights Dave had never been to, such as the World Trade Center and the Statue of Liberty. Sunday evening we went to see Roz, who was getting ready to leave for college. I was glad to see that she and Dave seemed to have put any remnants of animosity behind them.

On Monday morning Dave came with me to Barnard to register for my classes. This was a very important moment for me. I guess it was because my parents, who had never been able to attend college themselves, had always stressed the importance of a good education, and because I knew that my going to a school like Barnard was the fulfillment of their dreams. At any rate, I felt that, in a way, I was going to college for them as well as for myself. The magnitude of this overwhelmed me as I walked into the registration building, and I actually felt myself shiver.

"Isn't this wonderful?" It was with a sense of awe that I whispered the words to Dave.

He looked at me and laughed. "What's so wonderful? After going to college for a while, you'll find it's a school like any other. There are good professors and bad; you'll get a lot out of some courses and nothing out of others. If you get all jacked up about it, you're bound to be disappointed when reality sets in."

His words hurt. While everything Dave said about college was probably true, going there was still something special to me, and I didn't like being put down. I concentrated on filling out my schedule and getting out of registration as soon as possible.

When we got outside I was able to put aside my injured feelings. Dave, whose parents and older brother had all gone to college, took his education for granted. He couldn't possibly be expected to understand how I felt about it. Besides, it was too nice a day to waste time sulking. Dave had brought his camera, and we decided to go down to the park by Riverside Drive and take some pictures near the Hudson River and the George Washington Bridge.

It was a mistake to go down the drive with Dave, because it was a place Lenny and I had gone to often in the past, and it was filled with too many memories. Dave and I found a secluded spot in the woods where we could be alone. I closed my eyes as he kissed me and struggled to chase all thoughts of Lenny and the city out of my mind. All I had to do was to recapture some of the magic of New Hampshire, and everything would be all right.

We kissed awhile, and then I lay back in Dave's arms, looking at the sky and the great gray bridge that spanned the river. My eyes focused on some tiny figures way up on the bridge, and I gasped. Even from this distance I could recognize them. It was Lenny, Sheldon, and two of their friends, Billy Upton and Joel Fudd, probably having the time of their lives spying on Dave and me!

"Will that boy ever let me alone?" Angrily, I sprang to my feet.

"What's wrong?" asked Dave bewilderedly.

"Lenny" was all I said as I pointed to the bridge above.

"That rotten jerk thinks he can ruin it for us, doesn't he?" Dave got up and shook his fist at the faraway figures. "He wants a show, let's give him a show!" He grabbed me and started kissing me with exaggerated passion.

But I didn't enjoy putting on a show for anyone. "Come on, Dave, let's go back home. He can't watch us if we're sitting in my room."

Dave agreed reluctantly. He knew we'd never get into anything serious in my house with my brothers running in and out and with my parents' strict rules about things like no closing doors or sitting on beds. But Lenny had succeeded in taking all fun out of being down the drive.

When we got back to my block we found that Lenny was one step ahead of us. He and his friends were standing on my corner by the candy store awaiting our return.

"Hey, where did you dig up a stumpy little guy like that one?" Joel, who had an angelic face but a real fresh mouth, called out.

"She dug him up from Boston; that's where they grow nothing crap like that," Sheldon answered him.

"Hey, Stumpy! Want to come over and fight like a man?" Billy, who was tough and had a mean streak in him, challenged.

"He doesn't have the guts to do it!" added Lenny.

Dave, trembling with rage, made a move toward them, but I grabbed his arm. "Don't go over there, Dave. That's exactly what they want you to do. There's four of them and one of you, and Billy's a crazy maniac aching for some action. Ignore them and come upstairs with me—please!"

Dave made a move toward the corner but thought the better of it and followed me into my hall. "Okay for this time, Linda; I'm doing what you ask," he said, his face flushed and angry. "But make sure Lenny understands that if he pulls something like this next time I'm in, he's not going to get away with it. You're my girl now, and he'd better come to accept it."

"Dave, I thought I made it clear to you that at this point I don't want to be anyone's girl," I reminded him.

But Dave put his arm around me and kissed me as if he didn't even hear what I was saying. I felt totally out of control of the situation. This wasn't what I had had in mind when I had decided I needed freedom.

Chapter

Eight

THE FOLLOWING SUNDAY I WOKE UP WITH THIS HEAVY knot in my stomach I couldn't explain. It took me a moment to realize that this was the day of Lenny's nineteenth birthday, the first birthday in four years we wouldn't spend together.

I didn't know why this should bother me so much. I was so angry at Lenny for the scene he had made when Dave was visiting that I had been keeping away from him as much as possible. I was doing so well in my resolution not to think about Lenny that I even amazed myself.

But now I found I couldn't get Lenny out of my mind. I kept thinking about other birthdays we had spent together—his and mine. We always went out of our way to do something to make the day special for each other. It didn't seem right that I shouldn't be able to at least wish him a happy birthday. I went outside, determined that if I happened to run into Lenny, I would be especially nice to him.

I didn't run into him in the park or the schoolyard or the candy store, the usual places the kids hung out on a nice weekend afternoon. Instead of giving up, as I probably should have, I became all the more anxious to see him. I decided to head toward the poolroom on the chance I might run into him there.

The poolroom was the old-fashioned kind—dirty and sleazy, up a flight of stairs. It was a place where the boys in our neighborhood loved to get together and hang out until late at night. We girls rarely went there—the boys didn't like it if we did, and it wasn't an atmosphere we enjoyed being in anyhow. I slowed my steps as I approached the door to the poolroom. I didn't want to go inside if I didn't have to—it would look too much as if I were chasing after Lenny. He would know right away that the only reason I would show up there would be to search for him.

As I got near the entrance the door opened, and out came Joel Fudd. My heart quickened. If anyone knew where to find Lenny, it had to be Joel.

"Hi, Joel!" I said. "It's been a long time since I've had a chance to speak to you."

"Don't blame that on me," Joel replied harshly. "It's you who cut yourself off by breaking up with Lenny."

"Actually, it wasn't I who broke up with him," I explained. "He broke up with me because I wanted to be free to date other people. But it doesn't pay to get into that now. I was wondering if you happened to know where Lenny might be today. I—er—I wanted to tell him something."

"Yeah, he's up in the poolroom. Spent the night there, in fact."

"He spent the night there?" I repeated in dismay. "Oh, no, Joel. Don't tell me he's fighting with his mother!" Before he left for the navy Lenny often stayed in the poolroom all night when things got so bad at home he couldn't go there to sleep. It would be awful if this was happening again.

"Yes." Joel confirmed my fears. "Lenny feels he needs some time to look around for the right job, but his mother is tired of waiting for him to get himself together. She wants him to take something right away."

"But—but if he gets the wrong job, he'll never last in it," I protested. "He'll wind up quitting and being back in this same situation again and again."

"How nice for you to be so concerned about me." Lenny's voice dripped sarcasm. I looked up, startled to find he had come down the poolroom steps without my even noticing.

"Well, I am concerned. I told you I wanted us to still be friends." I tried to sound cheery. "That's why I thought I'd wish you a happy birthday."

"Happy birthday—that's a laugh," he said bitterly. "This has probably been the worst birthday of my life. I'm completely exhausted from being out all night, and I'm not even going to try to go home tonight until I'm sure my mother's fast asleep."

"It's a gorgeous day. Why don't you go somewhere where you can take a nap outside?" I suggested. "Like Fort Tryon Park, for example. I'll even go with you, if you like."

"You will?" Lenny seemed to perk up a bit. We said goodbye to Joel and walked together to the park.

It was a good half-mile walk from the poolroom to Fort Tryon Park, but it was so beautiful there, it was worth the effort. We sat in a secluded spot, set off from the rest of the park by a thick clump of trees and bushes. Lenny stretched himself out on the grass and laid his head in my lap.

"This is wonderful," he breathed. "The first real relaxation I've had in days."

"I'm glad," I said, hoping the emotion I was feeling could not be detected in my voice. Physical contact with Lenny was getting to me. I felt that energy, that mysterious force that had drawn me to him so many times in the past. I looked down, and he appeared to be on the verge of sleep. He looked so sweet, innocent, and vulnerable, I couldn't resist stroking the hair that tumbled over his forehead.

"Hmm. That feels good," he murmured. "I could almost pretend that you still like me."

"You don't have to pretend. I do still like you—although your behavior at times really gets me furious."

"Oh. You mean like that little scene I set up for Stumpy's benefit?" he laughed. "Wait until you see what happens next time he comes in!"

"Lenny!" I shoved his head off my lap. "How could you be so immature? Dave acted like a real gentleman when you came up to New Hampshire!"

"Well, that's *his* problem! I intend to do everything in my power to let him know that while he's up at school I'm right here in the city with you. It's only a matter of time until you realize it's really me you love and say goodbye to Stumpy for good!"

"Oh? And what makes you so sure of yourself?" I demanded hotly.

"This," he whispered, and before I knew what was happening he was kissing me on the lips.

"Don't!" I tried to push him away, but he persisted.

"Come on, it's my birthday," he said pleadingly.

The kiss had already weakened me. I couldn't resist him, although my head knew it would be better if I did. But after all, it was his birthday. I wrapped my arms around him and kissed him back.

Lowering my resistance was the worst thing I could have done. Once I had kissed Lenny and felt that powerful magnetic attraction that still existed between us, it was very hard to keep him out of my mind. I kept thinking about him, wondering about what he was doing, worrying if he was getting along with his mother or finding a job. One day I spotted him from a distance, deep in conversation with some girl I didn't know. Sheldon mentioned to me that Joel was seeing someone new and that he had fixed Lenny up with one of her friends. After that I couldn't help wondering how I would feel if Lenny fell in love with someone else.

Once school started it was easier to keep my mind off Lenny. I was busy with learning the routine of classes, finding my way around campus, getting to know my teachers and what they expected of me, and meeting new kids. I was still in awe over the fact that I was actually in college. I liked the intellectual atmosphere and the fact that the teachers treated us as adults, expecting us to be responsible for our own work without checking up on us. College was much more difficult than high school had been, and I really had to concentrate and work hard to get good grades. I took my schoolwork very seriously. I was there to learn, and I wanted to learn everything I could.

Of course, this didn't stop me from looking around

at the boys in my classes. I had not yet met anyone I was interested in, but I knew that it was important for me to develop relationships with other boys if I wanted to maintain my resolve to keep my distance from Lenny. After all, having the freedom to date others was a main reason I had broken up with him in the first place. Dave tried to write, call me, and come to see me as much as possible, but it wasn't enough. I was still much too vulnerable to Lenny.

The next time Dave got to the city was about two weeks after school had started. He grabbed me and kissed me as soon as he got off the bus.

"Did I ever miss you!" he said, gazing into my eyes with love.

"I missed you, too," I answered awkwardly. I felt uncomfortable at not being able to return the obvious intensity of his feelings.

We walked to my house together, Dave talking to me excitedly about the plans he had made for the weekend. I began to relax. His plans really did sound great.

On Friday night we went to see a movie, and on Saturday afternoon we went out to the Bronx to visit Perry. It was great to be with Perry again and away from the influences of my neighborhood.

Saturday night Dave took me to a party at a fraternity house in downtown Manhattan. It was Alpha Epsilon, a branch of the same fraternity he belonged to in Boston, and Dave had a friend, Paul, who had transferred to school in New York and was a member here. It was he who had invited us to come to the party.

"Hi, Dave! Great to see you!" Paul was very friend-ly as he greeted us at the door. "And this must be

Linda. I've heard so many wonderful things about you!"

"You have?" I was surprised.

"Yeah. I couldn't believe it when Dave told me he was thinking of following in my footsteps and transferring to New York, even when he told me it was because he'd met this fabulous girl. But now that I've seen you in person, I can start to understand why. And having good old Alpha Epsilon right here in the city will help him make the adjustment just fine! Why don't you two go into the party room, taste some of our fine food and drink, and listen to some of our fantastic music? I'll introduce you to the regulars; they'll make you feel at home."

The guys at Alpha Epsilon did make us feel at home, and it really impressed me that Dave was part of such a great fraternity. We danced together all night, and being there in his arms, gliding across the floor to the music, made me recall what was best about my relationship with Dave. We fit together so well and so smoothly; there was never the stress and tension, the wild ups and downs I had with Lenny.

But even as we danced I found there was something troubling me about Dave. I brought it up to him in the cab as we rode home from the party.

"Dave, how come you said that to Paul about transferring to school in the city?"

"How come? Because I wanted to find out what fraternity life was like in New York before I arranged to transfer here. Having gone through the process himself, Paul's the one to tell me what I need to know."

"You mean you're still thinking about transferring? You really want to do that?"

"Of course I do. This is no way to live—not seeing you for weeks at a time. It's going to get worse once I get loaded down with schoolwork, too. I probably won't get to see you now until you come up to Amherst for homecoming weekend in October. After that, I'll be lucky if I can make it to New York once before Thanksgiving, and after that, I won't see you again till Christmas vacation. Those are all great times to look forward to, but it's not enough, Linda. I want to be with you all the time. I can't stand it when we're apart. I'm ready to apply to school in New York right now!"

"But Dave," I protested, "I thought we had an agreement. We were going to wait and see how things developed before you did anything drastic like transfer schools. If you came to New York, it would mean a commitment between us I'm not ready to make. I still need time to be free, to date others, and to completely work out my feelings about Lenny."

"Lenny?" He jerked his arm from around my shoulder and looked at me intently. "Don't tell me he's still in the picture. You haven't been dating that lousy bum again, have you?"

"No-oo," I said slowly. "But that's not to say I never would. And he's not a lousy bum—he just still hasn't straightened out all his problems."

"My, aren't we being defensive of Lenny tonight?" Dave said sarcastically. "And here I thought you'd have him out of your system by now, for sure. What's he been doing, chasing after you again?"

"As a matter of fact, he hasn't. I only saw him once since the last time you were here—for his birthday."

"For his birthday. How cute. And did you give him a birthday present?"

"No, of course not. I just—" I stopped myself in time to avoid divulging how I had spent Lenny's birthday.

But Dave wouldn't let the matter rest. Sensing that something was going on between Lenny and me, he badgered me until I finally admitted I had kissed Lenny for his birthday.

"It was only a kiss; it didn't mean anything," I swore. And then I got annoyed at myself for having to defend myself to Dave. "Look, Dave, I never promised you I wouldn't see Lenny—or other boys, for that matter. I told you from the beginning that I need a period of freedom before I commit myself to anyone. That's why I don't want you to think about transferring yet. It's too soon for me to know what I want."

"Well, okay. If that's the way you feel about it." Dave pulled away from me and sat in the corner of the seat with his arms folded sulkily. He stared out the window and wouldn't say anything to me for the rest of the ride home.

I wasn't used to seeing this side of Dave, and I certainly wasn't used to this style of fighting. Lenny and I would get angry, yell, and have it out until we resolved an issue, but we never went for long periods of time without speaking. I couldn't stand the tension between Dave and me. I decided to try to make up with him.

"Come on, Dave." I grabbed his hand as we walked up the steps to my apartment. "You're leaving tomorrow morning, and it's stupid to spend our last hours fighting. I do care about you, I do. You've got to give me some time, that's all. Everything will work out if you just give me some time."

He turned to me with a look of hurt and desperation. "You don't leave me very much choice, do you? I love you too much, Linda, and that's my problem."

I felt so sorry for him that I threw my arms around him and kissed him on the lips. "You can't love anyone too much," I said softly.

But later on, as I lay in bed thinking over the evening, I realized what I had said wasn't really true. It *was* possible to love someone too much. I had felt that way about Lenny many times in the past, when he had done things to hurt me and our relationship, but I still kept coming back for more. At times like those, my love for him was damaging to me—I really was loving him too much.

It wasn't like that for me and Dave, though, I told myself. I would never willingly do anything to hurt him, so he couldn't be loving me too much.

I didn't know then what was in store.

If I thought I had escaped Lenny that weekend, I was mistaken. He was there on my corner, leaning up against the window of the candy store and eating a slice of pizza as Dave and I left my apartment the next day on our way to the bus station.

"Hey, Linda, want to finish my crust?" he called to me laughingly. He was referring to a private joke we had between us because of the fact that he never ate the crust of the pizza, so I would always finish it for him.

"No thanks, Lenny," I said nervously. I hooked my arm through Dave's and began walking quickly up the block.

"Aw, come on, Linda. You hate to see waste. I'll save it for you. You can come eat it after you dump off Stumpy."

Now I could see exactly what Lenny was doing. He was using the pizza to make Dave think that as soon as he left on the bus Lenny would be there to move in and take over. It was a cruel and rotten thing to do!

"I won't want it then, either, Lenny," I called out to him. "So don't bother to be around."

But Lenny was around. He followed us to the bus station and waited in hiding until the bus pulled into the street. Then he jumped out, making sure Dave would see him, and with a sadistic grin he slowly waved goodbye.

I saw the helpless look on Dave's face as he watched Lenny from the window. He was leaving, and Lenny would be with me, and there was nothing Dave could do about it.

The bus pulled out of sight, and I furiously stormed across the street to where Lenny was standing. "You have no heart at all, Lenny Lipoff! How could you be so mean and cruel?"

"It comes easily," he said, laughing. "Especially when I'm dealing with Stumpy. There's something about him that draws out every mean and cruel bone in my body."

"Well, it seems your body is full of those," I said hotly. "And I want no part of them, or any other part of your body, either!" I whirled around and stalked away from him.

"Is that so? Somehow I didn't get that impression last time I was with you," he said, following after me. "Or are my lips the only exception to that statement?"

I stopped short. "You really are something, Lenny! You make me sorry I ever try to be nice to you!"

"It always pays to be nice, my sweet," he said,

grabbing my hand. I tried to shake away, but his grip was too strong for me. "Now calm down. I've got some news I think you'll be happy to hear."

"Oh, yeah? And what would that be?" I ceased my struggle.

"A job. I went to an employment agency Friday, and they think they have the perfect position for me. They're trying to set up an interview for me next week."

"Next week? Then the job is far from yours, Lenny. Talk to me after you get it."

"Well, truthfully, I was hoping to get a bit of incentive from you. To help me decide whether or not to take it."

"Incentive? Like what?"

"Like a promise to go out with me. After I'm working and have some money to pay for our date, of course."

"I'm not promising anything, Lenny. It all depends on your behavior between now and then. And besides, isn't there some other girl you'd rather go out with now? Some friend of Joel Fudd's I heard about?"

"Uh-oh. It sounds like someone's been talking to you about June." He laughed. "That's purely a good-time situation. Means nothing."

This unwanted picture of Lenny making out with another girl flashed into my mind, and it bothered me far more than I wanted to admit. I blinked my eyes to chase it away. "So you don't need me to go out with after all, Lenny. As long as you have your 'good times,' what else could matter?" I was angry enough now to pull my hand out of his and make my escape up the block.

Linda Lewis

"What a temper!" he called after me. "On second thought, I'm not so sure I want to go out with you anymore, anyhow!"

This time he didn't chase after me. Part of me was glad about that, but part of me was very disappointed.

What was there about Lenny that could still get to me this way?

Chapter

Nine

I T WAS IN EARLY OCTOBER, WHEN THE TREES WERE CLOAKED in colors of autumn splendor, that I went to homecoming weekend at U. Mass. This was an event I had been looking forward to for a long time. It was my chance to be with Dave and to see what a big weekend at a real college campus was like as well.

That Friday afternoon found me riding up on the bus with my nose pressed against the window. This was all new territory to me, and the scenery kept getting more and more beautiful. But even all the beauty wasn't enough to prepare me for how wonderful the University of Massachusetts turned out to be.

It was the perfect fantasy of what a college campus should be: ivy-covered buildings, spacious lawns, streets of quaint New England houses lined with towering majestic trees. The day was clear and sunny, and the sky a brilliant blue background for the vivid autumn colors. Pumpkins and bunches of Indian corn decorated every lawn.

"I bet you can't help learning in an atmosphere like this," I said to Dave as he drove me from the station in the car he had just gotten as an early twentieth-birthday gift from his parents. "It's so beautiful, it makes me sorry I didn't decide to go to an out-of-town college. I can't believe you'd even consider leaving a place like this to come to New York."

"It doesn't matter where I am. I'll be happy just to be near you." Dave stole a quick kiss while we were stopped for a light. "Of course, it would be even better if you would find some way to transfer up here with me."

I looked around the lovely streets and for a moment was filled with longing. I sighed. "I told you I couldn't do that, Dave. My parents can barely afford Barnard."

"Well, we'll have to stick with the original plan of my going to school in New York. If you missed me half as much as I've missed you, you should be ready to agree to that by now."

"Dave, please, let's not start that again. I keep telling you I'm not ready for a step like that. We'll see how things work out for next year."

His face fell. "Then I guess you haven't missed me much at all."

"I didn't say that, Dave. Of course I missed you!" I hated always having to reassure him. It made me uncomfortable, especially since it was true that if Dave was aware of how little time I spent missing him, he would be very unhappy. But there were too many things going on in my life now to devote much energy to missing Dave. I was busy with schoolwork and the baby-sitting and tutoring I did to make extra money. And then, of course, there was Lenny.

Lenny was still not working, and he would show up

at the corner candy store at least several times a week. At first I tried to keep away from him, but he was behaving himself so well that after a while I allowed myself to get into some deep conversations with him. After all, even if we weren't going together, he was still wonderful to talk to. We actually began getting friendly, and a few times he even came down to Barnard to meet me and sit in on some of my classes.

"I might as well get some exposure to education while I'm waiting for my job to come through," he told me laughingly when I asked him why he did that. "Besides, didn't I ever tell you that I enjoy your company?"

I couldn't deny that I enjoyed his company, too. I could have more fun doing nothing with Lenny than doing the greatest thing in the world with someone else. This realization disturbed me. Lenny still had problems, and I didn't want to get back into a situation where I became so involved with him that I would lose sight of the fact it was best for me to date others.

Then, two days before I left for homecoming, Lenny met me on the corner with some wonderful news. "The job! I got the job I wanted!"

"That's great, Lenny! Is this the job you told me about? The one from the employment agency?"

"Yes. The name of the company is Freight Consolidating—it deals with shipping, freight forwarding, tariff rates, and all that."

"Oh. I don't know the first thing about that field. I didn't know that you did, either."

"I don't, but I can learn. I love working with numbers. It's a great business, Linda. Manufacturers all over the country want to save money on shipping, and our company pools their merchandise together so they can get the best rates. The ICC—the Interstate Commerce Commission—regulates all this stuff, so it's really complex, and you have to know what you're doing and how to operate a computer. There's so much to learn that there's even a school for traffic managers. My boss told me the company would send me there if I worked out. Finally I've got a job with a future! And now that I'm respectable again, I want to take you out this weekend, Linda, to celebrate."

"Oh." I felt awful. I was so excited for Lenny, and now I was going to have to tell him about homecoming. "Uh—I'd love to go out with you, but unfortunately I already have plans for the weekend."

"Well, break them. This is something special."

"I can't. Homecoming is only this weekend, and I've got my bus ticket and everything."

"Homecoming? Is that one of those whoop-dee-doo, phony college weekends where everyone gets drunk and makes a jerk out of himself?"

"I wouldn't put it that way, Lenny. There's a parade with floats, and a big football game, and lots of parties, and—"

"Say no more; I've got the picture." His face flushed with anger. "You just have fun with your college boy, Linda. I've got more serious things to deal with, like making a living and getting on with my life. And I'm sure I can find someone else to celebrate with while you're up there in fantasy land." He turned on his heals and stalked away.

Fantasy land. It was strange that the words Lenny had used so disparagingly turned out to be the very words that entered my mind to describe homecoming weekend at U. Mass. The houses on the blocks nearest the campus were all fraternity and sorority houses, and in front of each one was a float constructed for the football parade. The streets were filled with college kids, laughing and calling out to one another as they put the finishing touches on the floats.

"Here we are—Alpha Epsilon house," Dave announced as we pulled in front of a large clapboard house surrounded by a huge porch. It was already growing dark, and he took me on a quick tour of the house before depositing my things in one of the rooms that had been set aside for visiting female guests. He introduced me to my roommates for the weekend, Shelly and Robyn, and to the fraternity brothers who lived in the house.

"So you're Linda. I've heard so much about you." I kept hearing that remark whenever I was introduced to someone new. Finally, after the dinner that the guys fixed for us was over and the party for the evening had begun, I managed to get Robyn alone in a corner of the large living room long enough to ask her what it was that she had heard.

"Why, that Dave's madly in love with you," she told me. "And that he's planning on marrying you as soon as possible."

"Marrying me?" I repeated in amazement. "Is that what he said?"

"Well, I couldn't swear for sure that he said it. I only heard it secondhand. Tom, my date for the weekend, told me one of his brothers is so crazy in love he's ready to quit school and get married. The brother he was talking about was Dave."

"Quit school and get married! But Dave wants to be an attorney. That means years more of school. He couldn't have said that. He couldn't!"

Robyn looked at me as if I were crazy. "I don't know why you're getting so excited, Linda. I'd be pretty flattered if Tom said something like that about me. Besides, I told you what I heard was secondhand. If you want to know the truth, why don't you talk to Dave? Here he comes now."

I looked up, and there was Dave approaching. "They're playing one of our favorite dance numbers from the summer," he pointed out to me before I could ask him anything. "Let's get up there and dance!"

"Okay." I let him take me in his arms. It was amazing, but as long as we were dancing, that old magic clicked between Dave and me. I could close my eyes and pretend I was still with him in the country, gliding across the dance floor as if the two of us were made to be together in each other's arms.

But the dance ended, and there was still the issue I had to clear up. "Dave, I need to talk to you. Is there somewhere we could go to be alone?"

"Sure, there's an enclosed porch down the hall. No one will disturb us there."

But as soon as we got to the porch he began kissing me with such passion that it didn't seem the time for a serious discussion.

After all, it was a long time since Dave and I had been alone together, I told myself. And he really had missed me. I figured what I had to say to him could wait until the next day.

But when Saturday came, there was no opportunity to speak to Dave alone. In the morning was informal breakfast—a chaotic affair with boys and girls jamming the kitchen, trying to cook eggs, pancakes, and bacon all at one time. Then it was off to the homecoming parade, and then the game itself. I understood basic football, but not the finer points of the game, so Dave was busy explaining the moves to me. Massachusetts won, and the spectators erupted with cheers of joy. Dave was in a terrific mood, and I didn't want to spoil it right then with serious conversation that could be put off until later.

Later was the big fraternity victory party. The boys built a fire in the fireplace and brought in pizzas, sandwiches, bottles of wine, and a huge keg of beer, and the celebrating began. At first it was fun. The guys took turns getting up and making funny speeches, toasting the school, the football team, and one another. But each toast meant another round of beer, and that meant the crowd was getting progressively drunker, louder, and more rowdy as the night wore on.

I wasn't big on alcohol. I didn't like the taste of beer, and a glass or two of wine was all I could handle without feeling sick, so I just held on to my same glass of wine all evening so I wouldn't look out of place. Dave showed no such restraint. He put away mug after mug of beer, keeping up with the biggest guys in the fraternity.

I wasn't very happy about this. Dave was starting to act silly, and he couldn't even dance right. The more Dave drank, the more he lost his sense of rhythm and style. He began leaning on me heavily, and his weight was too much for me to support.

"Let's forget about dancing, Dave," I said finally, pulling out of his arms. "I'll be leaving in the morning.

The weekend is almost over, and we still haven't had a chance to talk."

"Talk? Sure we can talk." He grinned drunkenly. "We'll go to the porch the way we did last night."

"Not if you're going to do what you did last night," I protested. "At least not until we really do have that talk."

Dave promised, so I put my arm around him and helped him down the hall to the porch. But as soon as we sat on the wicker sofa he started kissing me again.

"Come on, Dave. You promised!" This time I was firm in pushing him away.

"Whad's da mattah?" He slurred the words, a hurt expression on his face.

"I mean it about talking, Dave," I said. I decided to get right to the point before he hit me with another onslaught of passion. "I've heard rumors that you're telling people you're going to quit school and marry me. You don't mean anything like that, do you?"

For a response, Dave aimed another kiss at my lips, but I managed to turn away so that he only got my cheek. "Come on, Dave. I want you to answer me."

"Mean it? Of course I mean it. Ever since I met you, Linda, you're the only thing on my mind. I can't even concentrate on school anymore. My grades are slipping, and if they keep going down, I probably won't get into law school anyway. If I quit school and we get married, it'll be much better. Once we're together, I can finish school at night. Marry me, Linda. Say you will! I love you so much!" Having said these words, he started kissing me over and over again so that I could hardly get a breath of air, much less a chance to protest.

"Dave, stop!" I finally got out the words.

But Dave wasn't listening. He kept kissing me all over, moving his hands all over my body, pulling at my clothes and at his. That was when I realized where he intended this to lead. It was not what I wanted—not here, not with him in this horrible drunken state.

"No, Dave, no!" I increased my struggles. With great effort I managed to push him off me. I rolled away from him, looked up, and saw he was immediately coming back for more. Instinctively I swung out my hand and slapped him across the face.

Whack! The sound of the impact frightened me as much as it startled him. "You—you hit me!" He held his hand to his cheek in disbelief. "You hit me—you couldn't love me—you hate me!" He grabbed a throw pillow and threw it over his head, and I heard the sound of him sobbing into it.

"Come on, Dave, I don't hate you." Now that it was evident he wasn't going to attack me further, I felt sorry for him. Tentatively I put my hand on his shoulder. I could feel his body shaking with unhappiness.

Gently I stroked his back, his hair. The sobbing stopped. "Now, let's talk about this sensibly," I said, removing the pillow from his face.

But Dave would do no more talking that night. He had passed out there on the sofa, incapable of doing anything more than sleeping off his alcoholic binge.

I untied his shoes and took them off his feet, but I was not about to touch the rest of his clothing. Leaving him sleeping on the sofa, I went out of the room and closed the door.

* * *

In the morning I was so disgusted with Dave that I didn't even want to see him again. I stayed in my room talking with Shelly and Robyn until it was almost time to leave to catch my bus. I had gone down to the kitchen to find out about calling a cab when Dave made his appearance. He was still dressed in the clothes in which he had fallen asleep.

"Sorry I slept so late, Linda. I meant to get up early so we could have more time together, but I guess I had too much to drink last night."

"You certainly did," I said quietly.

"Boy, is my head ever splitting!" He pressed both hands to his forehead. "And foggy! I don't remember a thing! I hope I didn't say or do anything out of sorts."

"As a matter of fact, you did. You got very pushy physically. And you were saying all these crazy things about quitting school and getting married."

"I was?" He shook his head in disbelief. "Well, I'm really sorry about that—there's no excuse for acting that way. It just goes to show you, drinking too much can really get you into trouble. I hope you can forgive me, sweetheart. It wasn't really me doing and saying those things—it was the alcohol! I'll never drink that much around you again, I promise!" He went and poured himself a cup of black coffee and sat down at the kitchen table, looking up at me like a guilty puppy.

He looked so miserable and so sincere that I decided to forgive him. It was true that alcohol could make you do and say all sorts of crazy things. But there was still something I had to straighten out.

"I just want to clarify one thing with you, Dave. You're not serious about failing classes and quitting school, are you? You still intend to be an attorney, right?"

"Quitting school?" He gave a startled laugh. "Did I tell you that last night? Boy, I really must have been out of it to say something like that! I'm having a tough time in a few of my classes this term, but it's nothing I can't handle. And of course I still want to be an attorney. Do you think I'd do something dumb like blow my whole future?"

I put my hand on top of his and gave a sigh of relief. "I'm glad to hear you say that, Dave. Because you know that one of the things I most admire about you is that you've got your head together about school and are on your way to a good career. I've had so many problems in that area with Lenny that I certainly wouldn't want to have to go through that scene again with you!"

"Don't worry about that," Dave assured me. "I wouldn't let you down. As long as you love me, that's all the incentive I need to help me succeed!"

It didn't seem like the right time to remind Dave that I had never come out and told him I loved him, that I was still confused as to what real love was and exactly what I wanted.

"Just keep doing the right thing," I said. "That way things will work out for the best for everyone."

As he drove me to the station I noticed the weather had changed drastically overnight. The day was dark, chill, and drizzly, and a stiff wind had blown many of the colorful leaves off the trees. The beautiful floats had already been dismantled, and the kids that were out on the streets were hurrying to take shelter indoors.

I could see now that going to school at U. Mass. was no panacea. Parties couldn't go on forever; there was hard work and studying, hassles with teachers and roommates, fights and broken romances, too. When it came down to it, wherever you were, you still had to deal with reality.

There was no fantasy land.

Chapter
Ten

WHEN I GOT BACK FROM HOMECOMING WEEKEND I FELT absolutely drained. My relationship with Dave had seemed so simple when we were in the country; it had brought me nothing but pleasure. I didn't understand what had happened to complicate it so in the short time since we had returned home. Why was he talking about things like quitting school and getting married, things that I was far from ready for?

I still wanted a relationship with Dave, but I wanted it the way it used to be. I didn't know how to handle this new side of him. I was actually relieved that he wouldn't be able to come to New York for over a month; it would give me a chance to breathe and sort out my feelings.

As for Lenny, once I had turned him down for the date I didn't get to see him at all. I knew he was working and didn't have much time to hang around, but I also knew he could have made some time to see me if he'd wanted to. It seemed as if he were deliberately avoiding me. As much as I hated to admit it, I missed the time we had been spending together.

The week after homecoming I ran into Joel Fudd, who gleefully informed me that Lenny had taken out Lauren Blum instead of me on Saturday night. Lauren was one of the many girls who had made the mistake of allowing themselves to fall in love with gorgeous Joel, only to have their hearts broken. I had only met Lauren once, but that was enough to know she was very nice and not the kind of girl Lenny would take out just to have a "good time." I told myself I shouldn't care about this, but it made me a lot more unhappy than I wanted to admit.

"He's going out with her again this weekend," Joel seemed quite happy to add. "They're going to a party Sheldon's throwing on Saturday night."

"A party at Sheldon's? Sounds good. Maybe I'll show up if I have nothing to do," I told him.

"That would not be a good idea," Joel said bluntly.

I stared at him. Parties in our neighborhood were usually informal and open to any kids from our crowd who wanted to come. "Why not?"

"Because, as I told you, Lenny is coming with Lauren. I know for a fact he wouldn't want you there."

This got me really angry. "Lenny wouldn't want me there? Well, who is he to determine something like whether or not I can come to a neighborhood party?"

Joel laughed cruelly. "You might as well face it, Linda. Lenny's got a lot of power in this neighborhood. Everyone thinks what you did to him was pretty rotten. No guy who is a friend of Lenny's would ever come near you, and you're going to find yourself excluded from a lot of neighborhood events."

What Joel said made me feel awful. Although there

was no one in the neighborhood I was interested in romantically, I had hoped to be able to go out with some of the boys as a way to ease into the social scene. And now I was being totally shut out. It wasn't fair. I hadn't broken up with Lenny in order to hurt him. I had only done it because I had thought it would be best for me!

Saturday night found me sitting home alone, watching an old movie on TV. It was one of those romantic films, with soft music playing in the background as the camera focused in on the final kiss between the hero and heroine. I guess I shouldn't have watched anything like that because it made me ache with longing to have my love take me tenderly in his arms.

My love. Ha! I had to laugh bitterly at that, for now it seemed I no longer had a love. Lenny was on a path that led away from me; my feelings for Dave seemed to swing back and forth like a pendulum; and if there was someone else destined for me in the future, I had no idea where or when he might turn up. Maybe it was because I had been so used to having a boyfriend around me all the time that I felt lost without one. I wasn't sure. But the sad fact was that now that I had acquired the freedom I had wanted so badly, truthfully, most of the time there wasn't all that much I wanted to be free to do. Most of the time I was downright lonely.

. I worked myself up into such a terrible state of feeling sorry for myself that I had a hard time falling asleep that night. When I woke up on Sunday feeling just as rotten as I had on Saturday night, I knew it was time for me to seek some guidance. I went to visit my friend Fran Zaro and told her all that was going on in my life and how I was reacting to it.

"All this freedom I wanted doesn't seem to be bringing me the happiness I thought it would," I concluded.

"Freedom? Do you call what you've been doing freedom?" Fran demanded as we sat in the room she shared with her younger sister. Even shorter than I was, Fran had frizzy black hair, a pale, freckled complexion, and beautiful violet eyes that were usually hidden by thick glasses. But all Fran had to do was take off those glasses, and she was instantly transformed into someone very desirable. Fran had no problem getting boys interested in her. She played the field, dating one after another without getting involved with any of them—exactly what I thought I should be doing. She was the perfect one for me to go to for advice.

"What you need is to forget about both Dave and Lenny for a while," she said. "Turn your attention to other boys—go out with lots of them. Find out what the dating game is like. Stop being so serious and put some fun into your life!"

"Easier said than done," I said gloomily. "The boys in the neighborhood won't go out with me because they're afraid it would get Lenny angry. I've gotten to know a few boys in school, but none of them has shown any interest in taking me out. I feel like some sort of vulture, the way I've been looking at boys recently—always watching them, always wondering if anything might develop romantically with them—and I don't like the feeling at all. How do you go about getting boys to ask you out, anyhow? I've been out of practice in the dating game for so long, I guess I forgot how it's played!"

I sighed with discouragement and sank back on Fran's bed, staring at this painting she had received as a gift from one of the boys she went out with. It was this view of a starlit sky as seen from the inside of a cave. "You know, Fran, that painting pretty much represents how I feel about life right now—that there's light out there somewhere, but right now I'm stuck in the recesses of some deep, dark cave."

"Is that how you feel?" Fran laughed. "Come on, Linda! Cut this self-pity crap. It takes a while to get back into the swing of dating, but once you do, it gets a lot easier. What you need is some exposure—get out more, go to places where you're going to meet boys, and let them know you're available. Before you know it, they'll start asking you out. It's bound to happen—it's what happened to me!"

"Do you really think so, Fran?"

"Of course. All you have to do is be willing to open yourself up to other people. You remember Mike Marlin, this guy I've been going out with recently?"

"Of course I remember. I ran into you with him in the street just last week," I reminded her.

"Well, do you also remember the other boy who was with us, Jason Schultz?"

"Jason? Let's see. I know there was another boy with you, but I really didn't pay much attention to him. I can't even remember what he looked like."

"Well, he remembered what you looked like," Fran said. "He was definitely interested, but I didn't encourage him because I knew you were preoccupied with Dave and Lenny. But if you're ready to start opening up to others, I think there's potential here. In fact, Mike is taking me to a party next Saturday night.

Jason is invited, too, and I know he doesn't have a date yet. Do you want me to try to arrange something?"

"Arrange something? I don't know, Fran. I've never been on a blind date."

"It's not a blind date—you've already met the guy."

"But I don't even remember what he looks like!"

"That's not what matters, Linda. I won't try to tell you that Jason is gorgeous or anything, but he's a perfectly nice guy. I bet you'd like him if you gave him a chance. Come on, say you'll go along with this. We'll have fun, and it'll be exactly what you need to pry you out of your cave. What else do you have to do Saturday night, anyway?"

It was this last remark of Fran's that did it for me. She was right. I didn't have anything else to do. That was one thing I really missed about having a steady boyfriend—knowing I would have something to do each weekend. I hated spending so much time alone.

"Okay, Fran," I sighed. "If Jason is willing to take me to the party, I'm willing to go with him. See what you can do to fix it up."

Saturday night found me sitting on Fran's bed, gazing at my reflection in her bedroom mirror, and wondering why I had agreed to this half-blind date. I remembered how I used to look forward to my Saturday nights with Lenny, how I couldn't wait to be with him no matter what we were doing. Now my stomach was tied in a knot of nervous apprehension. I had no idea what the evening had in store for me. Would I like Jason? Would this date be the start of a new relationship for me? It was nice to fantasize that, but truthfully, it was much more likely that we wouldn't hit it off. What if I really couldn't stand the guy, or if he disliked me? What if we had nothing to say to each other, or if he had bad breath or an obnoxious personality, or if he was some sort of pervert? Oooh! All these "what ifs" were driving me insane! If this was what it felt like to be dating casually and "playing the field," I didn't like it one bit.

"Here they are!" Fran sang out merrily when the doorbell rang. I moved to get up, but she motioned that I should sit right back down again. "Stay where you are. Rule number one when dealing with guys is not to seem overanxious. My father will get the door and tell them we'll be right out."

I couldn't see the point of this but went along with it anyway. We wasted a few moments fixing our hair and checking our makeup, then went out into the living room where the two boys were talking to Mr. Zaro.

"Make sure not to bring the girls back too late," he said, his eyes twinkling good-naturedly in his ruddy face. Fran's father was the easygoing one of her parents. Whenever Fran had to ask for something she went directly to him. "It wasn't so long ago that I was a boy, and I remember all too well what it was like!" He laughed knowingly.

"We won't be late, Mr. Zaro," Mike said, his voice polite and serious. He was dark; his hair was neatly combed, his clothes carefully pressed. He looked like the kind of person who knew what he wanted and systematically went after it.

While this conversation was going on I had a chance to take a good look at Jason. Now that I was with him, I remembered him, but I wasn't at all surprised that I had forgotten what he looked like. He was so average-looking he was practically nondescript. His hair was brown, and his eyes, as best as I could make out behind his glasses, were brown as well. He was of medium height and build and had pasty-white skin and a slightly oversized nose. His personality was nothing to remember either. He said very little as Mike drove the four of us to the party.

It was a good thing that Fran was so chatty, I couldn't help thinking. If it wasn't for her, I don't think I could have come up with much to talk about with Jason, and he certainly wasn't contributing much to help the conversation flow.

But once we arrived at the party I no longer had Fran as a buffer. She introduced me to a few people she knew, then went off to dance with Mike. I was left standing there next to Jason, and I couldn't think of a single thing to say.

I looked at him, opened my mouth, and closed it again. I stared down at my feet and shuffled them a little, hoping he'd get the hint and at least ask me to dance. I looked up at him again. He gave me a nervous half smile, but still he said nothing.

I didn't understand it. Fran had said Jason was interested in me, but he surely wasn't acting that way. Why didn't he say something? Why didn't he ask me to dance? Didn't he know how to act with a girl?

That's when I realized that this might be the problem. Maybe Jason didn't know how to act with a girl. After all, Fran had told me he was interested in me, but he had nothing to show him that I was interested in him. It must be really hard for a boy to ask a girl out and take the chance that she wouldn't like him or would reject him. Maybe he was waiting for some sort of sign from me that I at least thought he was okay.

I smiled at him. "Do you like dancing?" I asked.

"Dancing? Oh—uh—sure! But I didn't know if you did," he said apologetically.

"I do."

"Oh—uh—good! Then will you—that is—do you want to?"

"Sure!" I let him take my hand and lead me out onto the floor.

Jason was a pretty good dancer, and I told him that when the song was over. That seemed to break the ice between us. We danced a few more dances and then went to get something to eat. I asked Jason about school, and he told me he went to Cooper Union in downtown Manhattan, where he was studying architecture. I had always found architecture fascinating and asked him some questions about it. That gave him the opportunity to really open up.

By the time we left the party I discovered I liked Jason. I wasn't attracted to him physically, but that didn't matter. For a change, it was nice to spend time talking to a boy on a friendly basis.

Unfortunately, I hadn't considered what might happen on the ride home. Mike was obviously in a romantic mood. Every time the car stopped for a red light he took Fran in his arms and started kissing her. I had a feeling they would do a lot more than kiss, except for the fact that the lights weren't long enough to get anything serious started. Still, it was disconcerting to be trying to carry on a friendly conversation with Jason in the backseat while all that passion was going on in the front.

Then I noticed that Mike had taken a turn that led away from Washington Heights. "Mike, you're going the wrong way," I pointed out.

"No I'm not." He turned around and grinned meaningfully. "The night is too beautiful to waste going straight home. I thought we'd stop by Fort Tryon Park and look at the river and the stars."

The river and the stars were fine to look at, but it soon became apparent that they were only an excuse for Mike to go after what he was really interested in. As soon as he parked the car he was all over Fran.

I didn't know what to do. This was not an atmosphere conducive to anything but sex. And while I had decided Jason was nice to talk to, that didn't mean I wanted to make out with him. Physically, he did not turn me on.

I sat there in the backseat feeling very uncomfortable. I just hoped that with Jason and me doing nothing in the backseat, Fran and Mike would have the consideration to get their making out over with fast. I also hoped that since Jason was the shy type, he wouldn't get up the courage to make a move on me.

My hopes amounted to nothing. Jason seemed to have interpreted my earlier friendliness as a signal that it was okay to get physical. Before I realized what was happening he had his arm around me. I didn't object to this; it actually felt nice to be snuggled up against him in the car.

I guess Jason figured my snuggling meant it was okay to go further. Without warning he took my face in one hand and turned it toward him. His lips pressed against mine, and his tongue forced its way into my mouth. It was so unexpected and so unwanted that I actually started to gag.

For a moment I couldn't catch my breath. I pushed him away, and he stared at me in shocked disbelief. I felt so embarrassed that I didn't know what to say to him.

That's when I panicked. I lunged for the car door and thrust it open. I was out of the car before anyone could stop me, running down a path through the park and into the bushes, running away from a scene I didn't know how to handle.

It didn't take me long to realize that running away wasn't going to solve anything. We were in a secluded area of the park and a good mile away from my house. Anyone could be hiding in the bushes. It was unsafe and insane for me to be walking alone at that hour. Besides, Fran had arranged the date; it wouldn't be fair to her if I disappeared without warning. I turned and headed back to the car, trying to think of something I could tell Jason to explain my irrational behavior.

I rounded a bush and bumped into a shadowy figure hidden in the darkness. My heart pounded with fear, and I instinctively closed my eyes, waiting for some horrible fate to befall me.

"Linda! What happened?" I opened my eyes and sighed with relief when I saw it was Jason.

"Jason!" I gasped. "I'm so glad it's you! I'm sorry for the way I acted. I really owe you an apology." Then, as we walked back to the car together, I came out with the truth about my behavior. I told him I had been going with one boy for so long that I was really inexperienced in the ways of dating. I told him that I hadn't been ready for it when he had come on so strong in the car, and my response had been totally involuntary. It didn't mean I didn't like him—I thought he was very nice. I hoped that he could understand.

Surprisingly, Jason did try to understand my situation. He stood outside the car talking to me for a long time. He put his arm around me, but he didn't try to push anything more. He asked me questions about Lenny, and I wound up telling him the whole story of our relationship, our breakup, and the problems I was now having with Dave. Jason turned out to be a good and sympathetic listener, but that didn't change the fact that the thought of making out with him positively turned me off.

"What was going on out there with the two of you?" Fran asked me when we finally got back to her house, where I was to spend the night.

We sat in her kitchen, drinking milk and eating chocolate chip cookies, and I told her the details of my reaction to Jason.

She burst out laughing when I described how I had bolted from the car. "Boy, you are something, Linda. You don't have to be madly in love with every boy you make out with, you know."

"Maybe not, but I have to at least be attracted to him," I said. "I can't force myself to do something that goes against me."

"It shouldn't go against you to make out with any guy as long as you think he's nice," she said. "It's really no big deal."

"Maybe not to you, but everyone's different," I told her. "I learned something from this experience. There really isn't such a thing as carefree, 'casual' dating.

Everything's got its complications, and you've got to be prepared for them."

"You mean like a Girl Scout—always be prepared?" She laughed at that. "I guess you're right, Linda. You can't force yourself to do anything that goes against you. But the fact that you weren't physically attracted to Jason doesn't mean you won't be to someone else. I still think dating a lot of boys is the best thing for you right now. Don't let this experience discourage you."

"I won't," I promised. "Next time I'll have to be better prepared."

Chapter

Eleven

THE FOLLOWING WEEKEND I DIDN'T SEE ANY BOYS, BUT I did keep busy. I spent the time with another of my friends, Jessie Scaley. On Saturday afternoon we went shopping, then we took a ride out to Queens to meet Marilyn, one of Jessie's friends from school. We all went ice skating together, and then Jessie and I slept over at Marilyn's house.

Jessie wasn't someone I ordinarily would have chosen to be friends with, even though she could be a lot of fun at times. She could also be snappy and sarcastic, and she had a tendency to lie, so I never felt I could completely trust her. I had become close with Jessie because she had gone steady with Sheldon Emory, Lenny's best friend, for over a year, and the four of us often went out together. But Jessie had started private school the term before and had met some boys there who treated her better than Sheldon did. Recently he had caught her going out with one of them and had picked a big fight with her over it, and they had broken up. Since Jessie was a free agent, as I was, I figured we'd have a lot in common.

Unfortunately, we had a bit too much in common. Marilyn fell asleep quickly, but Jessie and I were up late talking, and our conversation kept gravitating to Sheldon and Lenny. Jessie lived in Sheldon's apartment building and had become friendly with Sheldon's mother. Mrs. Emory had given Jessie some information that I would probably have been better off not knowing.

"It looks like both Lenny and Sheldon are into new relationships," she informed me. "Sheldon's going out with some girl from the Bronx named Peggy, and Lenny's dating Lauren, one of Joel's old girlfriends."

"I know about Lauren; Lenny's been dating her for weeks now. Did Sheldon's mother say anything specific about her?"

"Only that Lauren is simply adorable, and very nice. Oh—Mrs. Emory did say that she never knew Lenny was capable of treating a girl so well."

"Probably a lot better than he ever treated me," I said grimly. This talk of Lenny and "simply adorable" Lauren wasn't doing me any good. I tried to change the topic by asking Jessie about some of the boys she knew from school, but I hardly heard her answers. My mind kept focusing on this awful picture of Lenny holding Lauren in his arms, kissing her, touching her, and telling her he loved her, the way he once did to me.

When I finally did fall asleep, it was to dream of Lenny. He came galloping up to me on a big white horse, and he motioned for me to climb on and ride with him. I reached for his hand, but just as I was about to grab it, along came this girl whose face I couldn't see, and she shoved me aside. It was she who climbed up and rode off with him, leaving me to stare after them, all alone with nothing but the aching emptiness I felt inside.

The letters and phone calls I got from Dave after homecoming were all sweet and proper as could be. He apologized over and over again for any behavior that might have been upsetting to me. He swore that nothing like that would ever happen again. I wanted to believe him. I wanted all those wonderful feelings I had had while with him in New Hampshire to come back to me. I didn't think I had felt really good about anything since I returned to the city.

The next week something happened to give me a lift. One of the boys I was friendly with in my modern European history class, Alan Bethel, asked me out to a concert given Saturday night at Columbia. Alan and I had often had long discussions after class about such topics as the reasons for Hitler's rise to power in Germany, and I had found him very knowledgeable. I was really looking forward to my date with him.

My parents were tremendously impressed with Alan, especially since he took the trouble to talk with them about our history class before we left for our date.

"A Columbia boy, and such an intellectual—it's wonderful!" my mother whispered to me as Alan began discussing the causes of World War II with my father. World War II was one of my father's favorite topics, and the two of them became so engrossed in their conversation that I practically had to drag Alan out the door so that we wouldn't be late for our concert.

I had never been to a formal classical music concert before, and I was impressed. Everyone was all dressed up and sophisticated-looking. I had worn my best dress, and I felt very important and proper as I sat next to Alan, waiting for the concert to begin. The program said the music would all be by the famous composer Wolfgang Amadeus Mozart.

"Did you know Mozart represents the climax of late-eighteenth-century music?" Alan asked. "He was a boy genius, born in Salzburg, Austria, in 1756, and began composing when he was five years old." Alan went on to fill me in on some background material of Mozart's life, his death before his thirty-sixth birthday, and the details of his most famous quartets, symphonies, and operas.

It was all very interesting, and I probably would have really enjoyed the concert, except for the fact that Alan had this annoying habit of humming along to the music, which he seemed to know by heart. He was so loud that I noticed several people in the surrounding rows throwing dirty looks our way. Alan, however, seemed oblivious to anyone else's needs, because he kept right on humming. I slunk down in my seat as far away from him as I could manage, in the hope that no one would know that I was with Alan. If someone I knew from school spotted me with him while he was humming away, I would never get over the embarrassment.

I felt a great sense of relief when the concert finally ended and we left the auditorium without running into anyone I knew from school. But the rest of my date was even harder to deal with than the concert had been. Alan suggested we go to a restaurant not far from the campus to get something to eat. As we waited for our order he talked on and on about the historical background of Mozart's times. This king and that king, this war and that minister—after a while it was all the same to me. I had had my fill of intellectualism for the evening. How I longed for some plain, ordinary conversation!

All my efforts at changing the topic amounted to nothing. It was fast becoming obvious to me that while Alan was absolutely brilliant as far as history was concerned, he was practically incapable of talking about anything else. I found myself starting to nod off as I attempted to listen to him drone on and on. I was so bored, I couldn't wait for the night to finally end.

Alan took me home by taxi. He sat with his arm around me, and this sick feeling came over me as I realized he might very well want to make out with me when he got me home. I didn't know what I would do if he tried anything. When I had talked to Alan at school I had actually thought he was pretty cute, but now, sitting so close to him, I was much more turned off to Alan than I had been to Jason. To make things worse, I was well aware that while I didn't have to see Jason ever again if I didn't want to, I had to face Alan every time I went to history class. I didn't want to act in a way that would ruin our friendship, but the thought of kissing him was making me absolutely ill. I didn't know if I could bring myself to do it.

I took a deep breath. How different this was from dating someone I really cared about! When I was with Lenny or with Dave, I couldn't wait for them to kiss me. I hadn't anticipated these kinds of annoying problems that were involved with casual dating, and I still didn't know the best way to handle them. I could only hope that Alan would decide to let me out of the taxi and that he would stay in it and keep right on going home.

That wasn't what Alan had in mind. The cab pulled up in front of my house, and Alan leaned over to pay the driver. "It's a good thing you live near Broadway. I can always find another cab to take me home," he said to me. He gave me a meaningful grin, and I knew I was in for trouble. In the greenish light from the street lamp his skin looked sallow, and his lips and nose looked absolutely huge. He totally turned me off.

"Right." I looked at my courtyard and was tempted to make a mad dash up the stairs to my apartment, to rush inside and slam the door behind me. But I couldn't do that. I didn't want to be rude to Alan or hurt his feelings in any way. I had told myself I needed to be prepared. I decided the best way to handle the situation was to brace myself to kiss him as briefly and painlessly as possible and come up with some excuse for having to go inside fast.

I never had a chance to see how this would work. Alan and I had just gotten out of the taxi, which was waiting for the light to turn green, when an old, red, familiar-looking Chevrolet pulled up behind it. It was Billy Upton's car, and in it were Lenny and all his buddies—Billy, Sheldon, and Joel.

"Well, well, if it isn't Linda." Billy leaned out of the window and grinned malevolently.

"And look what she dug up to go out with tonight!" Lenny laughed. "Where do you get these little pukes from, anyhow?"

"The sewer. This one looks like he came from the

sewer—a regular sewer rat!" concluded fresh-mouth Joel.

"Hey, sewer rat, you'd better keep away from that girl before you get yourself exterminated!" threatened Sheldon. "She's the personal property of my friend here, isn't she, Lipoff?"

Alan stood there throughout as if petrified. He looked at the boys, then at me, then back at the boys once again. "I-I didn't know she was anyone's g-g-girl," he stammered. Then he pulled open the door of the taxi. "I-I think I might as well go home in this cab, Linda," he called to me as he slid inside. "You can never tell when I'll find another one. See you in school!"

"In school!" I waved after him. The light changed, and he was gone. I stalked over to Billy's car, where the boys were rolling around, laughing hysterically. As grateful as I was to have gotten out of kissing Alan, I was furious at the boys for pulling such a stunt. What if I had been out with someone I really cared about?

"You guys have a lot of nerve!" I said angrily. "What do you mean ruining my date like that?"

"Ruining your date?" Joel demanded. "From the looks of that guy, we did you a favor, Linda!"

"I never saw anyone make a move as fast as the one he made toward that taxi!" Lenny was laughing so hard he had to hold his stomach to get the words out.

The boys looked so funny that I had to struggle to keep from laughing myself. I didn't want them to think I condoned their actions in any way. "What are you guys doing driving around here on a Saturday night, anyhow?" I asked. "Don't you have anything better to do—like going out with girls? That is, if there's anyone who'll have you!"

"For your information, we did have dates for to-night," Lenny made sure to let me know. "And Lauren—or any of the others, for that matter—would put that creep you went out with to shame! We just took the girls home and happened to be riding down your block on the way to the poolroom. So don't go thinking we came here looking for you!"

"I don't waste my time thinking any thoughts about you whatsoever!" I told him. Then I turned around and headed for the entrance to my building as fast as I could.

I didn't want Lenny to see how upset I was. Why did it bother me so much that Lenny was still going out with Lauren? Why did the realization that he had been seeing her far too long for their relationship to be a casual one make my stomach feel like it was all tied up in knots?

Chapter

Twelve

I COULD HARDLY SLEEP THAT NIGHT—I WAS BUSY HAVING arguments with myself in my head. The sensible part of myself told me I had no right to be upset by the fact Lenny was dating another girl. Even though he was the one who had actually done the official breaking up, he had only done so because I had found Dave and no longer was willing to go steady. And it was right for me to go out with other boys—I needed the experience. I was too young to commit myself, especially to someone as unsettled as Lenny.

Despite all this fine logic, the ache in my stomach at the thought of Lenny and Lauren wouldn't go away. I longed to see him, to kiss him, to hear him say that Lauren didn't matter and that he still loved me and would take me back the moment I told him I was ready. When I finally did fall asleep, it was to the memory of what it had felt like to kiss him that day in the park.

I awakened the next morning to the sound of the

telephone ringing. "Linda, it's for you!" my mother's voice called out.

Maybe it's Lenny, I couldn't help thinking as I ran to the phone. But the voice on the line belonged to Jessie Scaley.

"Hi, Jessie. What's up?" I asked.

"What's up is a broken window in my room. Would you believe someone threw a rock through the glass last night? Shattered it to pieces and nearly scared me to death in the process, too!"

"Oh, how awful! Were you hurt?"

"No, but I could have been. Some of the glass landed only a foot from my bed."

"Did you see who did it?"

"No, but I have a pretty good idea. I ran to my window in time to see the back of a car turning around the corner. I couldn't read the license plate, but I could see the color. The car was bright red, Linda. Now who do we know who'd be out driving around the neighborhood at one in the morning in a red car?"

"The boys!" I gasped. "They were riding around in Billy's car when I came home about twelve last night—Billy, Lenny, Joel, and Sheldon. But why would they do a terrible thing like throw a rock through your window?"

"Just to be mean and rotten. You know Sheldon's been really miserable to me since we broke up. Well, last night I had a date with this guy Troy from school. Sheldon knew about it, and I bet the boys were driving by to see if they could catch him taking me home. When they saw my light was on in my room, they knew they had missed me, got angry, and threw the rock to scare me."

"So you think Sheldon's the one who did it?"

"Absolutely not. He'd be too chicken his parents might find out, since they live in my building. It was one of the other three—Billy, Joel, or Lenny. But I'm not going to waste my energy trying to find out which one. I'll let the police do that."

"The police! Don't tell me you're involving the police in this!"

"My mother called them right away. This is serious, Linda. Do you realize that if that rock had hit me in the head, I could have been killed? My mother wants the boy who threw the rock found and punished, and so do I. I called you because I thought you might know who was in that car last night with Billy, and you told me exactly what I needed to know. Thanks, Linda. Now the police will know exactly whom to question. I'm going to tell them to start with Lenny. It's my opinion he's the one!"

She hung up the phone, and I was left all upset by what she had said. Was Lenny capable of doing something as awful as throwing a rock through Jessie's window? If he had and was caught, it could blow everything for him, including his new job. I had to speak to him before the police did!

Quickly I dialed Lenny's number. His mother answered the phone. She had never liked me, and I hated having to speak to her, but I had to warn Lenny. I apologized for having disturbed her and asked if I could please speak to Lenny.

"He's still sleeping. He had a date last night with this darling little girl," she made sure to inform me.

"I know. Could you please wake him up anyway? I

wouldn't bother him, but this is extremely important."

"Well, if you insist," she said with annoyance. "But make sure you tell him this is your idea, not mine."

"I will." I waited impatiently till Lenny came to the phone.

"Linda? What is it?" He sounded groggy and grouchy.

"I can't tell you on the phone, Lenny, but it's important that you leave your house immediately. Come meet me somewhere. I've got to talk to you *now.*"

"What's so important that you can't tell me on the phone?"

"It has to do with the police, Lenny. Now will you come and meet me?"

I guess the word "police" did it, because Lenny agreed to meet me at Bigfoot's, the diner he and the boys often went to late at night because it was always open. "Just give me some time to wash up and get dressed," he said.

"No problem. I've still got to get dressed myself. See you there."

I raced to get ready, and after explaining to my mother, who had a hard time dealing with the fact that I was leaving the house without "nourishment," that I was having breakfast out, I ran the five blocks to Bigfoot's. It was located right between Lenny's house and mine.

Lenny used to live closer to me, but while he was in the navy his mother moved to a larger, nicer apartment in a better area located about ten blocks away. He must have been really upset by what I had told him, because he was already there, sitting at a table and eating the breakfast special—eggs, bacon, and two slices of toast—when I arrived.

"Want some?" He gestured to his food.

"No, thanks. I don't feel like anything. What I have to tell you is too important." I launched right in to the details of Jessie's call. "And the worst is that she's telling the police you're the prime suspect," I concluded. "They're probably trying to contact you for questioning right this minute."

Lenny, who loved to eat, had not taken a single bite the whole time I was talking. He punched his fist down on the table. "I told him not to do it!" he said angrily.

"You told him? Then it wasn't you who threw the rock?"

"Me? You should know me well enough to realize I'd never do a thing like that, Linda. I might fool around and play jokes on people, but I could never do anything that might injure someone."

He looked so hurt when he said this that I couldn't help but put my hand on his. "I didn't really think you would, Lenny. But Jessie thinks you did, and that's what she's telling the police. That's why I wanted to talk to you—to warn you so you could decide what to say when they called you for questioning."

"I'd say the truth. That there are plenty of people in the neighborhood who dislike busybody Jessie. They can try questioning someone else."

"But you were there, weren't you? You know which one of the boys did it. If it wasn't you, it must have been Billy, Sheldon, or Joel. They were the only other ones in the car."

"They were when you saw us, but it so happens we took on some other passengers right after we left your block. One of them really had it in for Jessie. We had stopped in front of her window to talk about her, and he worked himself up into such a state that he picked up a rock from the street and threw it before anyone could stop him."

"But why? I mean, it would have to be something pretty awful to get a person so mad."

"It was. Jessie said some things to this guy's girl that led to her breaking up with him. That's all I'm going to tell you, Linda, because I don't want you to know who it was. But a guy can get pretty crazy over losing his girl. Believe me, I know."

"Oh." I felt so awful when he said that to me that I kept on holding his hand. "I'm really sorry, Lenny. I never wanted to hurt you, you know. I just had to do what I thought was best."

"I know, I know. I've heard all that stuff before," he said bitterly as he pulled his hand away. "I'll tell you what. I'll let you make it up to me by coming with me to Jessie's and backing me up while I explain to her that it wasn't I who threw the rock."

"It's a deal!" I grinned. "And one more thing, Lenny. If you don't mind, I'll take you up on your offer of sharing your breakfast with me before we go. Suddenly, I'm starving!"

I went with Lenny to Jessie's. Using his verbal gifts of persuasion to the fullest, he managed to convince her, her mother, and the police officer they called on the telephone that he was not the one who had thrown the rock. We left Jessie's and stood outside her house talking for a while. Somehow, this incident made me feel closer to Lenny, and I was reluctant to leave him. But the November day was cold and windy, and a few drops of rain were already beginning to fall. We weren't going to be able to stand outside talking much longer.

"So what are you doing for the rest of the day?" I asked, hoping he might come up with something that included me.

"Nothing much. I was just going to go home and watch the football game. My mother's going to New Jersey to visit my aunt and uncle, so it'll be peaceful in my house for a change. What are you doing?"

"Nothing." I shrugged. "I thought maybe you'd come up with a good suggestion."

"Well, you could come and watch the game with me."

"Okay," I agreed, knowing full well what I was setting myself up for.

It seemed perfectly natural that Lenny took my hand and held it as we walked together to his house—I had forgotten how right it felt to have him do that. It seemed perfectly natural that he put his arm around me as we sat on the sofa to watch the football game—after all, he had always done that when we watched football together in the past. And it seemed perfectly natural to kiss him during the commercials, to touch him and to have him touch me. Before I realized what was happening we were carried away on a wave of passion so intense that nothing could have stopped it. It was wonderful, the way it had always been before.

Afterward, I sat there holding him, scratching his back the way he liked me to. I couldn't believe what had just happened. I certainly had never intended the day would go that way when I woke up in the morning. But I couldn't really say I was sorry. The contrast of how right it was to be with Lenny compared to how wrong it had seemed with other boys made me realize something. No matter how much I tried to fight it, I couldn't seem to stop loving Lenny completely.

"I hate to tell you this, but sometimes I think I still love you after all," I whispered.

"I always knew you did," he said, stroking my hair. "It was only a matter of time before you got Stumpy-boy out of your system and came back to where you always belonged. You can call him and tell him the news right now from my phone. I want to be there listening when you tell him you're through."

This got me angry. "Wait a minute, Lenny. I didn't say that I wouldn't go out with Dave anymore. Whether I love you or not, I'm still not ready to cut out the other people in my life. I need more time to be sure of how I feel about everything—and to make sure you're really headed on the right path this time. Besides, Dave has plans to come in next weekend for his birthday. I can't tell him not to come!"

He pulled away from me angrily. "Oh, so it's Stumpy-boy's birthday, is it? And you can't tell him not to come? Isn't that too bad? I see you haven't learned anything from all this, Linda. You still think you can have your cake and eat it, too. Well, I told you before, you can't have it both ways. I have a date with Lauren for next weekend, which I was actually considering breaking for you. But now you can forget it! Lauren is worth two of you any day! So you might as well go home now, Linda. The football game is over!"

He got up from the bed, shut off the TV, and stood

there glaring at me with a hostility that was frightening.

"Okay, Lenny, if that's the way you want it!" I tried to look self-righteous as I prepared to leave his house. But this horrible feeling inside me told me I had just blown everything.

Chapter

Thirteen

I DIDN'T SEE LENNY ALL THAT WEEK, BUT HE WAS ALWAYS on my mind. I thought of him even as I went shopping for Dave's birthday gift—a set of bongo drums I knew he wanted. The day was chill and drizzly, and even the fact that I found exactly what I wanted without a hassle was not enough to raise my spirits.

I was struggling back home with the drums when I ran into Fran Zaro in the street. "Fran! You're just the person I need to talk to!" I would have hugged her if it wasn't for the bulky package I was holding.

"Let's go up to my house if you want to talk," she suggested. "It's freezing out today!"

"What are you dragging around in the package?" Fran asked as we warmed up in her kitchen over large mugs of hot cocoa.

"Bongo drums; I got them for Dave," I told her. "It's his birthday, and he's coming in this weekend to see me."

127

"Oh. So I take that to mean all is going well with you and Dave?"

"Well, I guess so. I mean, we haven't had any problems recently in our letters or talking on the phone, but that's mainly because we've been avoiding discussing sensitive issues. I won't really know how I feel about Dave until I see him again. In the meantime, I find myself constantly thinking of Lenny. It's awful!"

"Uh-oh. Sounds like you're heading for trouble." Fran took off her thick eyeglasses, wiped them with a napkin, then put them back on and stared at me intently. "Let me take a wild guess, Linda. You're starting to get involved with Lenny again, and all your fine resolutions about having your freedom and getting to know and date other boys are falling by the wayside."

I looked at her in amazement. "How did you know?"

"I know you." She laughed. "Plus, I happened to run into Lenny in the street the other day. We spent some time talking, and he told me that he knew perfectly well that you loved him, but you still couldn't recognize what you wanted."

"Oh, he told you that, did he?" I felt a flash of hot anger. "He has some nerve! He's so darn sure of himself that he thinks he has me right where he wants me!"

"Well, does he?" Fran asked.

"I don't know," I admitted. "Oh, Fran, I'm so confused. You, Roz, my parents—in fact almost everyone I know—have been telling me for years that I shouldn't tie myself down to Lenny, and I realized you were right. When Dave came along it gave me the perfect opportunity to finally make the break with Lenny, but now complications are arising from him as well. Being involved with two boys is one of the most difficult situations I've ever found myself in. Dave keeps telling me he's madly in love with me, and I don't think I feel that way about him. Having casual dates with boys I don't care about is meaningless and frustrating. I've been doing it because I think I should, but I don't really enjoy it."

"Just because it didn't work out for you with Jason—" Fran began.

"It's not just Jason," I said quickly. "It's the whole dating scene that leaves me empty. You go out with someone and spend all this time worrying about how to act, what to say, and whether or not to make out with him. At the end of the night maybe you had a nice time or maybe you didn't. But you know what? If you aren't going to have a lasting relationship with the guy, it really doesn't make that much difference."

"It makes a difference to me," Fran protested. "I like to have fun with a boy."

"Okay. I grant you that it's better to have a nice time than not to. Basically I did have a nice time with Jason, until he started coming on to me, but that still isn't what matters. The fact remains that casual dating leaves me empty inside, because it's not what I really want."

"And what is it that you really want, Linda?"

I sighed. "Truthfully? Something very simple— knowing I have someone who is right for me, someone I love and who loves me back. I don't think this casual dating—going out with boys I don't really want to go out with because it's supposed to be good for me— works for me."

"Maybe you haven't given it enough time," said Fran. "Or maybe you really do love Lenny so much that dating others isn't for you. In that case, you probably should go back with him and forget all this stuff that's theoretically 'good for you.' Everyone's needs are different. You've got to be true to your own heart."

"Fran! I can't believe you said that! Weren't you the one who lectured me on the evils of going steady?"

Her face flushed. "Yes, but that was before Mike."

"Mike?"

"Uh-huh. We seem to be getting more and more serious, Linda. I've been seeing him almost every day recently. He told me he doesn't want me to go out with anyone else, and I'm ready to agree!"

"You—I can't believe it!"

"Yes, and now I can look at your situation with Lenny entirely differently. It's one thing to want to play the field when you haven't met someone special. But once you do, you really don't want to go out with anyone else."

"That's exactly how I used to tell you I felt about Lenny, but you never understood."

"Well, your situation with Lenny was always complicated by the fact that he had so many problems. But now that I feel so strongly about Michael, I can see how love can go beyond complications. You see, I have them with Michael, too. He comes from Michigan and will go back there to live after he graduates in June, which will definitely pose some problems for me. But I don't have to worry about that now. All I have to do is love him and be with him each day I can, and if it's right for us and meant to be, the future will take care of itself."

LOVING TWO IS HARD TO DO

My conversation with Fran left my head spinning. She made me realize that while most people might feel that it wasn't right for me to go steady with Lenny, when it came down to it, only *my* feelings counted. I was the one who knew how it felt to go on boring dates with boys I didn't really care about to prove I could do so; I was the one who knew how uncomfortable it was to deal with Dave when the gap in our feelings for each other grew wider each day; I was the one who knew how it felt to keep myself away from Lenny when my heart ached from wanting him. Under the circumstances, it didn't make sense for me to do anything but be with Lenny, the boy I really loved.

Once I had come to the conclusion that Lenny was the one I wanted, I knew I had to do something to reverse the separate directions our lives were taking. It was Thursday; Dave was supposed to be coming Friday; Lenny was supposed to be taking Lauren out on Saturday. The more he saw her, the more there was a chance he would really fall for her. There had to be something I could do to prevent that—there had to be.

I decided on a risky course of action. I would meet Lenny at the subway entrance when he got out of work that evening and see what his attitude was like. If he was willing to give up the date with Lauren, I would find some way to keep Dave from coming in.

I felt very nervous as I waited for his train to arrive. What if Lenny refused my offer? I would look like an absolute fool running after him.

I was about to change my mind and leave when I saw him approaching. He looked so good, all dressed up in a business suit, that I stood there as if rooted to the ground, staring at him. It was too late to leave; he had already seen me.

"Uh—hi, Lenny," I said in what I hoped was a casual tone of voice. "I thought I'd come by and see how you're doing."

"I'm doing fine," he said in a voice that dripped with ice. "All set for the big birthday weekend with Stumpy?"

"His name is Dave," I said with annoyance. Darn it, it was so hard to be nice to Lenny when he was in a hostile mood. "Uh—I was thinking, Lenny. About what you said last Sunday when we were together."

"What about it?"

"Well, maybe I could arrange it so Dave wouldn't come in—as long as you wouldn't be going out with Lauren, that is. I could tell him something like I got sick suddenly or whatever—"

"Whatever is that you tell him that you realized you love me and never cared for him at all and never will. That's what I want you to say."

"I couldn't do that, Lenny—it would hurt him too much! I want to let him down as easily as possible."

"There is no easy way to let down someone who loves you! When you're dealing with someone as crazy about you as Dave is, you've got to make it perfectly clear you're through with him, or he'll never leave you alone! It's all or nothing, Linda. The choice is up to you."

"I can't do that to Dave, Lenny. I just can't do it." I shook my head.

"Well, you sure didn't have any trouble doing what you did to me!" he said angrily. "Look, Linda, why don't you leave me alone? I'm perfectly happy now with the way my life is going without you—I'm finally starting to find myself. My health is better since I'm out of the navy; they love me at work, and I'm going to start traffic management school at night and really advance my career. But best of all is that I've found a nice, uncomplicated girl like Lauren to go out with. I don't need you coming around with your half-baked ideas to mess things up for me!"

He turned his back to me and walked away. Tears of hurt, anger, and frustration burned my eyes. So Lenny's life was fine without me; he didn't need me coming around anymore, and he was perfectly happy with Lauren. Was that the case? Well, I'd show him! Not only was I going to let Dave come in that weekend, but I was determined to have the best time with him ever!

Chapter

Fourteen

FROM THAT MOMENT ON, ANYTIME UNWANTED THOUGHTS of Lenny intruded upon my mind, I would banish them by substituting the image of Dave. I would picture the way it had been in New Hampshire, with Dave and me dancing to the music of the band or walking together under the beautiful starlit sky. How I longed for those wonderful, romantic feelings to be with me once again. I couldn't wait for Dave to come to the city. I was so eager to see him that I threw myself into his arms as soon as he got off the bus.

"Dave! I'm so glad you're finally here!"

"You missed me that much, huh?" He grinned broadly.

"That much. It's been really tough on me recently. I'm beginning to see that this whole dating scene is not nearly as fun and glamorous as people told me it would be. Truthfully, I really don't think it's for me."

"Linda! Does that mean you're ready to make a commitment? To settle down and be loyal to me?"

"I might be getting closer to that point," I heard myself say. "But I still need more time to be sure. It's so hard when you're so far away."

"That's exactly why I've been telling you I want to transfer to school in New York. It's pure torture being away from you, Linda. Now that I've met you, I don't enjoy going out with other girls. I don't even care about fraternity parties and stuff at school. All I can think of is how much I'd rather be with you. That's why I get drunk sometimes—to forget this loneliness that's eating me up inside because we're apart."

"Oh." I didn't know what to say to this. I couldn't tell him that I felt the same way about him, because it really wasn't true. My missing Dave was more missing the way it used to be—that simple, magical relationship we had had in New Hampshire. "I'm lonely a lot, too" was all I admitted.

"Then say you want me to transfer to the city, Linda," he begged. "There's not that much time left for me to get in my applications if I want to be accepted for next term."

"Does that mean you do want to finish school? You weren't serious about quitting and getting married?"

"Linda, Linda." He took my face between his hands and gazed into my eyes. "Sometimes I'm so crazy from wanting you that I actually think thoughts like that. But I know it wouldn't work. It's important for me to be a lawyer, if for no other reason than to make you proud of me. I fully intend to finish school—as long as I can be around you! What do you say?"

What did I say? I felt this tremendous ball of hot pressure in my chest at the thought of it. As much as I felt for Dave, as much as I loved the idea of having a future lawyer for my boyfriend, as much as I needed him to get Lenny completely out of my system, as much as I was already burned out with the dating scene, I still wasn't ready to make this commitment.

"Are—are you sure your parents wouldn't mind your going to a school so far away?" I tried to buy time by asking.

"Why should they? They're already paying to have me go to an out-of-town college. The fact that I'm transferring to one in New York City wouldn't make that much difference to them. They're more interested in making sure that I finish school, that I do what I need to be happy. And they know that what I need to make me happy is to be with you."

"Then you told your parents about us?"

"Of course. You're not just any girl to me, Linda. I want to marry you!"

"And you said this to your parents? What did they say?"

"They want to meet you. They would like you to come up to Boston for Thanksgiving vacation and spend some time with our family. Do you think you can?"

"I—uh—I don't know." The thought of spending all that time in Dave's house was frightening. What if his parents didn't like me? What if I didn't like them? It could be a very uncomfortable situation. Besides, I knew perfectly well that to go to Boston for Thanksgiving would take my relationship with Dave that much further in the direction of getting serious.

"Let's take one step at a time, Dave. I'm still not ready to commit myself to anyone, and I don't even know how my parents would feel about my being away for Thanksgiving. I'll talk to them about that and let you know before the end of the weekend."

I knew perfectly well that if I had told my mother I was missing our family Thanksgiving dinner to go somewhere with Lenny, her objections would be overwhelming. That's why I was so surprised that when I asked her about going to Dave's she put up no resistance at all.

I brought up the question late that afternoon as I was helping Mom prepare dinner in the kitchen. "As long as it's okay with Dave's parents, it's fine with me if you go there for Thanksgiving," she said calmly, not even looking up from the potatoes she was peeling.

This took me by surprise. "F-fine with you? You don't care that I won't be with the family?"

"Of course I care." Now my mother looked at me. "But your father and I realize that you're growing up now, and we can't hold on to you forever. We both like Dave and the fact that he's going to be a lawyer. It's important that you get to know his family. So I'm sure your father will agree with me when I say you can go."

"Oh. Thanks, Ma." This uneasy feeling in my stomach made me aware that I had probably been counting on my parents' opposition to get me out of going to Boston. I decided to hold off telling Dave that it was okay with them until I knew for sure that I wanted to go.

Dave and I had a great weekend together. He was thrilled with his bongo drums and played them for me in rhythm with tapes he had brought along of some of our favorite songs from the summer. We spent Friday

night at home, dancing together in my room, and my
parents even went so far as to let us close the door and
have some privacy. Saturday was warm for November, and we spent the day visiting Central Park and
the zoo there. At night we went to another party at the
Alpha Epsilon house.

Dave and I got along really well the entire weekend.
He didn't get drunk; he didn't bring up stuff I couldn't
handle like quitting school and getting married; he
didn't pressure me to come to Boston for Thanksgiving; he didn't do anything to get me mad. I was much
more relaxed with him than I had been at any time
since the summer.

Maybe it was the fact that Lenny kept out of our
way all weekend that helped. Or maybe it was the fact
that any time my mind turned to Lenny, I immediately saw a picture of him with Lauren, which would
cause a surge of anger so intense that it reinforced the
knowledge that I would be best off never seeing him
again. At any rate, I was beginning to think that my
recent revival of feelings for Lenny was nothing more
than some temporary insanity I had to go through to
get him out of my system. Maybe it was Dave I really
loved after all.

We got along so well that, as I walked him to the bus
stop, I gave him the answer he wanted to hear. "Okay,
Dave, I'll come to Boston for Thanksgiving."

He looked at me, his eyes aglow with love, and he
kissed me right there in the street. "Oh, Linda. You
don't know how happy it makes me to hear you say
those words. Now I can go ahead with my wonderful
surprise."

"Surprise? What surprise is that?" I asked.

"You'll find out at Thanksgiving. If I told you now,

it wouldn't be a surprise anymore, would it?" He laughed and kissed me on the lips.

"No, I guess not," I said a bit uncomfortably. I had this uneasy feeling that I might not find Dave's surprise quite as wonderful as he did. In fact, I felt uneasy about the whole idea of meeting Dave's parents and staying at their home.

I put those thoughts out of my mind. Dave had been so nice all weekend, and he had looked so happy when I said I was coming to Boston. He promised to show me around the city, which I had never seen, and that was something I could look forward to. I got myself so excited by the prospect of my visit that I hardly thought of Lenny. I began to think I could really be successful in prying him out of my heart once and for all.

I was scheduled to leave for Boston on the Wednesday afternoon before Thanksgiving. Then, Tuesday night, I received a call from Roz, who had just come in from Buffalo for the holiday.

"Hi, Roz! I'm so glad you called me before I left. I'm going to Boston for Thanksgiving, you know. Do you think I could get to see you tomorrow before I leave?"

"That depends." Roz's voice sounded strangely subdued. "You see, I have to spend all tomorrow at Fran's."

"The whole day? But why?"

"Oh, it's awful, Linda! Mrs. Zaro just called—you know she and my mother are close friends? Well, it seems Mr. Zaro had a sudden heart attack. He's dead, Linda! The funeral will be tomorrow afternoon."

"Oh, no, Roz!" I couldn't believe it. It had only been a few weeks since I had seen Mr. Zaro, red-faced, healthy-looking, and joking away as usual. "How could this have happened to him so fast? Poor Fran! Poor Mrs. Zaro! What can I do to help?"

"Well, you can come to the funeral tomorrow and to the house afterward to give some moral support. That's all anyone can do."

"I'm not sure I can even do that," I said. "I'm supposed to leave for Boston tomorrow afternoon, remember?"

"Well, if you can't come, you can't," said Roz. "We all have our priorities. It's up to you."

"Maybe I can change my arrangements," I told her. "If I left on Thursday morning, I could still get to Boston in time for Thanksgiving dinner, and I could go to the funeral, too. I'll call Dave about it now."

"Do that, Linda. I know it would mean a lot to Fran if you were there."

I called the bus line and found there was a bus leaving early enough on Thursday for me to make dinner. Then I called Dave to let him know what had happened.

I didn't expect Dave to give me so much trouble about changing my arrangements. "I had something special—that surprise I told you about—planned for us for Thursday morning. If you don't come Wednesday night, you're going to ruin it all," he said.

"I'm sorry, Dave, but this isn't something frivolous that came up. It's a death. Fran is one of my very best friends, and I want to be there for her. I can still get to your house for Thanksgiving dinner, and that's what counts."

"Not to me. I'm not going to go begging you or anything, Linda, but this surprise means everything to me. It's something I've bought for you, a symbol of our future together. But I've got to have enough time with you so we can discuss our plans and how we're going to announce it to everyone at dinner. It's essential that we have Thursday morning to do this, or everything will be ruined!"

Maybe I didn't want to know the truth, but at that point I still hadn't figured out what it was Dave was talking about. "What exactly is this 'everything' that will be ruined, Dave? If you expect me to miss the funeral of one of my best friends' father, you're going to have to be more specific about explaining why."

"Do you have to be so obstinate, Linda? Can't you just accept my word for it?"

"Not when you're asking me for something like this, Dave. Come on, now. I'm a big girl, and I don't need to have surprises. Tell me what it is that's so important."

"Us. Our whole future together. Whether I'm happy or unhappy. Whether my life can go on."

"Dave! You're talking in riddles, and I'm losing patience. Will you please come out with it and tell me what this surprise is?"

He sighed deeply into the phone. "All right. But I'll always remember it was you who took the romance out of this moment. The surprise is a ring, Linda. A beautiful diamond engagement ring I bought for you. I planned to ask you to marry me when we were alone on Thursday morning and announce it to the family at Thanksgiving dinner."

"Engagement ring? Marry you?" I was so stunned I could only repeat the words.

"That's right, Linda." Dave's voice on the phone was breathless and excited. "I know this isn't a romantic way to ask you to marry me, but you left me no choice. I figured if we got engaged now, we could plan the wedding for next June, after I graduate from college. I'm sure my parents would help us out while I'm going to law school, and we both can work part-time until you graduate. It'll work out; it'll be wonderful, as long as we can be together. Say you will, Linda. Say you will. I love you so much!"

My head was absolutely spinning. This had been such a difficult day—first the news about Fran's father, and now this unexpected proposal from Dave. I didn't know what to say to Dave. He claimed he loved me, but his love had become so obsessive, so consuming that I no longer felt it was really love at all.

When I had first met Dave I had thought he was so perfect—a clean-cut, handsome college boy who had his life and priorities in order and a great future as a lawyer. I had never foreseen all the complications that would arise from our relationship. The problems I had with Dave were different from those I had with Lenny, but they were problems just the same. It was only now that I was allowing myself to see Dave as he really was—so self-centered and involved in his own little fantasy love affair with me that he was oblivious to the emotions involved in something as significant as a death. How did I even think I could love someone who lacked so much, not only in feelings for others, but in feelings for me as well?

Dave always said he understood and accepted my needs, but when it came down to it, he never really had. If he did, he would never have bought a ring when he knew I was not ready to make such a commitment, when I had made it so clear to him I still needed time for freedom and had no intention of getting engaged. He would never be putting on such pressure for me to miss the funeral and come up to Boston when he wanted me to.

I realized all this, but I was still not ready to let go of him. "Look, Dave, I still haven't changed my mind. I'm not ready to get engaged or to make any other commitments. Why don't we forget all this serious stuff and have a nice, pleasant Thanksgiving weekend? I'll come up there on Thursday for dinner, and you can show me around Boston, and—"

"Show you around Boston?" he interrupted. "Are you crazy, Linda? I just asked you to marry me, and you're treating me like some sort of tour guide! Forget it. I regard this as a test of your feelings for me, and there's no room for flexibility. I'll be at the bus stop waiting for you Wednesday night at the time we originally agreed upon. If you're not there, forget it!"

Before I could say anything further he hung up the phone, leaving me staring at it, not knowing what to do.

No sooner had I replaced the receiver than the phone rang again. I was sure it was Dave calling back, and I was not ready to speak to him further. Still, I picked it up. "Yes?"

To my great relief, it was not Dave's voice I heard, but Lenny's. "Hi. I just heard some terrible news and thought it would be better if I was the one who broke it to you," he said solemnly.

"If it's about Fran's father, I already heard it from Roz," I told him.

"Oh. Then I suppose I'll see you at the funeral tomorrow."

"The funeral? Don't you have to go to work tomorrow?"

"Yes, but I'll arrange to take a few hours off in the

afternoon. My boss is a real human being. He'll understand when I tell him Fran is someone who has been close to me for years."

"Yes, anyone with a heart should be understanding when it comes to death," I told him. Then I paused a moment to think over what I had just said. If Dave had any kind of heart, he should come to his senses and forgive me for not coming to Boston when he wanted me to. It was right for me to go to Fran's father's funeral, and that's what I was going to do.

Chapter

Fifteen

I HAD NEVER BEEN TO A FUNERAL BEFORE. IT WAS VERY SAD. Mrs. Zaro and Fran and her younger brother, Arthur, and sister, Susan, were all crying throughout the service. I felt so bad for them. I couldn't imagine anything worse than having someone so close to you die.

How awful it must have been for the Zaros to know they would never again see the person they had loved and shared their lives with and depended on for so many years. Mr. Zaro's death was so sudden, so unexpected. One day he was alive and joking, the next day he was gone. It made me aware of how fragile life was, and how precious. Much too fragile and precious to waste doing things that went against your true nature.

After the funeral everyone went back to the Zaro house to pay respects. I was glad I was there for Fran when I saw how many kids who weren't as close to her as I was had shown up. There were friends from school and friends from the neighborhood, and of course there was Mike. He held her hand and never left her side, unless it was to bring her something to eat or drink. You could see by the way he looked at Fran and treated her how much he cared for her.

"Boy, is Fran lucky to have someone who loves her at a time like this," I commented to Roz.

"Everyone's lucky to have someone to love them at all times," Lenny replied, having overheard. "Only not everyone's smart enough to appreciate it."

I stared at Lenny, and the meaning of what he had said hit me hard. There was nothing that could replace the kind of feeling that Fran and Mike had for each other. A casual date would never be here at a terrible time like this—it wouldn't even mean anything if he was. I tried to think of who I'd want with me if someone in my family had died, and I knew the answer immediately. Dave might have a great future as an attorney, but when it came to compassion and understanding, Lenny had it way over him. There was no comparison when it came to their personalities and the way I felt when I was with them, either.

I watched Lenny. He looked so handsome dressed in his best suit. He was talking to Fran, telling her a story about an old lady named Mary who worked in his office. Mary was always cold and went to shut the windows every time Lenny opened them to get some fresh air. Lenny would wait until Mary wasn't looking and sneak over to open the windows again, causing her to flip out and go crazy in front of the entire office. His description of Mary and her actions was so vivid and so funny that Fran actually managed to laugh.

Lenny had such a wonderful way with people, I couldn't help thinking. When he wanted to, he knew exactly what to say to make them feel better. And he had made such great strides recently in getting his life together, despite the difficulties he still had at home.

That was the moment that everything came clear to me. I couldn't deny it any longer. Lenny was the one I wanted, and it was time I did something about it.

I asked Lenny to walk me home when we left Fran's. It was a bit awkward being with him, as we were still affected by the somber mood of the funeral, and our usual light, teasing interchanges seemed out of place. Besides, there were many unresolved issues between us. I knew I was ready to give up Dave for him, but he didn't. And I didn't know if he was ready to give up Lauren.

"Well, I guess I won't be seeing you for a while," he said as we reached my building. "I hear you're going to Boston for Thanksgiving, but I can't say that I hope you have a good time." I could see the bitterness in his face as he turned to leave.

I grabbed his wrist to stop him. "I'm not going to Boston."

"You're not?" He turned back to me. "Why?"

"Why don't we go somewhere where we can talk, and I'll tell you," I replied.

We walked together to Haven Avenue, the last street by the Hudson River, and sat up on the wall that overlooked the river and the great gray span of the George Washington Bridge. It was a spot of great significance to Lenny and me—it was there that we had first revealed that we liked each other; it was there that we had many times shared feelings and hopes and pain.

It was almost sunset. The day had been cold and

gray and wintery, but now there were some breaks in the clouds through which the dying rays of the sun managed to shine, painting the sky with strokes of fiery oranges and reds. The autumn wind blew briskly off the water, but for a change I wasn't chilly. I guess it was because my insides were burning with what I had to say. I knew it wasn't going to be easy, and I was afraid of Lenny's reaction. But it was the time. I had no choice but to tell him how I felt.

He was watching the river, watching the sunset. I gazed at his profile, taking in every detail, his forehead gently sloping to his fine, straight nose, his long lashes, his lips I had so often kissed. I saw pain and tension etched into his face, and I felt awful to know I had been the cause of it. I longed to reach out and touch him, to caress away his pain, but I didn't dare. I didn't know how he would react to me. He was so close and yet so far away.

I took a deep breath and began to speak. "What I wanted to tell you, Lenny, was why I decided not to go to Boston."

"Okay, tell me." His voice was still hard and cold. He wasn't making this any easier for me.

"Well, the first thing I want you to understand was that I never planned for anything like this to happen to us. I met Dave in New Hampshire, he went after me, and I was flattered. I was attracted to him, and he seemed to have all the qualities you were lacking—stability, dependability, a prestigious career. I listened to other people and let them convince me that was important. Plus, I guess I did need a period, of freedom to find out how empty the dating scene was so I could see life more clearly. And now this death has come along to show me the way things really are."

"And what way is that?"

"Well, to begin with, I understand now that while Dave may be doing well in school and have a successful career all lined up, that's not what really matters. A career is only what a person does for a living, and it's not what you do but who you are that's important in life. Dave's always had it so easy he doesn't know how to handle things when they don't go his way. The way he reacted to Fran's father's death showed me that he's lacking as a person. He actually ordered me to miss the funeral and come to Boston this afternoon, or not to come at all."

"So the fact that you're here means you're not going at all?"

"That's right. And that I'd really rather spend the time with you—that is, unless you have a date with Lauren or something." I could hear my heart actually pounding as I waited for his reply.

"Lauren? No. I wasn't planning on seeing her because she's going to her grandparents' for the weekend."

"Oh? And what about after the weekend?"

"Well, to tell you the truth, Linda . . ." He paused and stared at the water, and I could tell he was enjoying keeping me in suspense. "It was getting pretty boring going out with Lauren. You see, she spent half the time talking about Joel and how unhappy she was since he broke up with her, and the other half of the time . . ."

"Yes?" I couldn't stand the pauses anymore. "Go on, Lenny. Please."

"The other half of the time I'd be saying the same kind of things about you!" Lenny couldn't help grinning when he said this, and it was the first indication to me that I might be forgiven.

"Then you still want me? You can forgive me for what I've done?" I held my breath, waiting for his reply.

"Want you?" His voice cracked. "I never stopped wanting you. But how do I know that you're really ready to want me?"

"I'm ready, Lenny. I learned a powerful lesson from all this. Life's too short to waste time doing what other people think is right for me to do. It's time I stopped listening to everyone else's advice and paid attention to what my own heart is saying."

"Your heart?" Lenny turned to look at me, and I felt a surge of hope that gave me the courage to go on.

"That's right. My heart's been trying to tell me what I needed to know for a long time, but I refused to listen because I was convinced that dating Dave and other boys who are headed for terrific careers was right for me to do. But now I realize that it can't be right to deny what your heart knows. You've got to be true to yourself first, or things can never be right."

"And what is it that your heart's been telling you, Linda?"

I looked into his eyes, which were glowing with the light of the setting sun, and I was drawn to him by that powerful magnetic force I could never explain. There was no one else that made me feel that way—no one. I was so in love with Lenny. How could I have kept myself from seeing it for so long?

"That I love you, Lenny. I always have, and I always will."

He took me in his arms then and kissed me, a kiss so intense that for a moment I thought my soul had left my body and joined with his.

I belonged with Lenny, and only with Lenny. I would never fool myself into thinking I loved anyone else again.

Epilogue

LENNY WAS THE ONLY ONE FOR ME, BUT THAT DIDN'T mean everything went smoothly from that point on. For one thing, freeing myself of Dave was not as simple as I thought it would be. Even after I sent him a strongly worded letter I kept getting calls, letters, and even a surprise visit from him as he attempted to beg, plead, convince, and threaten me to come back to him. Each time I heard from Dave it rekindled those hurt feelings the relationship with him had created.

Still, Lenny and I got through it together, as well as the major problems we still had with parents, school, work, health, friends, and the minor unexpected difficulties that everyday life seemed constantly to throw our way. Each obstacle we managed to conquer served to bring us that much closer together and make our love grow that much more.

True to form, when we finally did get married, it was under the most difficult of circumstances. But that's a whole other story, and one that I might decide to tell someday. What's important to know now is that, despite the problems, difficulties, and obstacles, we made it. Lenny and I are still together and still loving each other today.

About the Author

LINDA LEWIS was graduated from City College of New York and received her master's degree in special education. *Loving Two Is Hard to Do* is her ninth novel. She has written six other Archway Paperbacks about Linda in the following sequence: *We Hate Everything but Boys, Is There Life After Boys?, We Love Only Older Boys, My Heart Belongs to That Boy, All for the Love of That Boy,* and *Dedicated to That Boy I Love.* She has also written two books about Linda for younger readers, *Want to Trade Two Brothers for a Cat?* and *2 Young 2 Go 4 Boys,* which are available from Minstrel Books. Ms. Lewis now resides in Lauderdale-by-the-Sea, Florida. She is married and has two children.